Kelly Creighton facilita
community groups and
include: *The Sleeping Seas*
with Girls (Sloane book
Hurricane and *Three*
anthologised and has been noted in many poetry and
short fiction prizes. She co-edited *Underneath the Tree*: an
anthology of Twelve Christmas Stories from writers in
Northern Ireland. In 2014, she founded The Incubator
literary journal, showcasing the contemporary Irish short
story. Kelly was the recipient of a 2017/18 ACES Award
from the Arts Council of Northern Ireland. She lives
with her family in Newtownards, County Down.

kellycreighton.com

@KellyCreighto16

ALSO BY KELLY CREIGHTON

POETRY
Three Primes

FICTION
The Bones of It
Bank Holiday Hurricane: short stories
(co-editor) Underneath the Tree

DI SLOANE BOOKS
The Sleeping Season
Problems with Girls

Everybody's Happy

stories

Kelly Creighton

incubator editions

First published in 2021
by Incubator Editions
Belfast

Copyright © 2021 Kelly Creighton

The moral right of the author has been asserted.

All characters and events in this publication, other than those clearly in the public domain, are fictitious and any resemblance to real persons, living or dead, is purely coincidental.

All rights reserved.

No part of this publication may be reproduced, stored in a retrieval system, or transmitted in any form or by any means, without the prior permission in writing of the publisher, nor be otherwise circulated in any form of binding or cover other than that in which it is published and without a similar condition including this condition being imposed on the subsequent purchaser.

ISBN: 9798623323552

theincubatorjournal.com
@IncubatorThe

Contents

The Supper   page 3

Provision   page 9

Other Children   page 21

Fear   page 33

Recompense   page 49

Regarding Jack Henry   page 69

Black Ice   page 95

Forever Home   page 113

THE SUPPER

I'D BEEN THERE by myself for nearly two months and hadn't said more than two words to anyone. I wonder if you can guess which two. When I attempted anything more, locals asked if I was Swedish or Finnish, trying to attune their ears. They were not as used to my accent as I was to theirs, despite the fact we spoke the same language.

Naturally, I had heard *them* on TV all my life. Theirs were movie voices, song voices. Even local singers from back home removed vowels or elongated them to sound like they were from *there*. But I always preferred when someone sang and you could hear their place of origin, especially if it was Scotland or Ireland. Funnily, over there they never took me for Scottish or Irish when I used that one phrase on repeat.

Apart from it I had no vocabulary, and when I asked for a bap (or was it a roll?) it was no longer called a bap (or was it a roll?). No, not there. There it was a *breakfast sandwich*. And weren't they right? The name was self-explanatory. There, locals called a spade a spade, they were phonetic, didn't sex up their spelling. As people, they are sure of who they are.

But you know I didn't go there to meet anyone. I went for the land.

'What's to see *there*?' an official at customs asked me.

He was so sure of himself it made me claim I didn't know.

'Then why are you going?' he asked.

I could have said I was a geologist and was going to study earth, it was the truth after all, and there wasn't a more interesting soil in all the world. Also true. But I couldn't say that. Working class girls like us don't always put ourselves forward.

I could have said I was going to some lectures by a visiting Australian geologist but I knew I wouldn't, and when I got there all I wanted to do was stay in bed.

There were solo expeditions, but not many, during which I studied the earth, took samples and photos, marvelled how anything still grew when the land was like dust.

Then I would go back to my room, climb onto my hotel bed and watch TV, then shower for dinner and thank some politely bored server for my meal, then thank them for my drink, then thank them for every refill thereafter, and for my dessert. If I had one that day. If I hadn't bought some salty, sweet treat from reception instead that I couldn't abide.

That night I sat alone in the hotel's rooftop bar looking out over the flat friable land and low-roofed buildings all around and I listened to the taped music playing, thinking how amazing it was that I used to listen to the same songs with you when we drove around, or when I cooked. When I used to cook. When I had you to cook for. I remembered that my mother, our third wheel, said she hated our music for what it sounded like, not understanding that how it sounded was one of the last things we liked about it. But we weren't about to explain.

It amazed me listening to those songs and being so far away and yet I could feel you so closely, and you, I imagined, could feel me. But I don't think it works that way.

There were times when I would call you and say, 'Just thinking about you … ,' and you'd say, 'Emerson, I'll have to call you back.'

There were other times we played charades and you mimed that your choice was *a movie* and I said, '*Apocalypse Now?*' before you'd even given a clue, and you shouted, 'Yes! Yes!' though both of us had never seen it.

I cracked the glass eye of my crème brûlée and listened to the next song. Again it was one of ours, and the next. Were we so mainstream? I wanted to call you but couldn't, and if I could and you'd said you'd have to call me back … well, I just don't know. Would it have been such a good thing? To know you would. Get back to me.

That night I forced myself out of the hotel, seeking noise.

In the square, people were gathered: families, kids playing, people talking. I wanted to speak.

I sat on the wall and listened as a woman was coaxed up to the bandstand to sing. She was game but tone-deaf as she belted out *Ob-La-Di Ob-La-Da*.

I have no recollection of you that I can hold against that song. I wonder if you have ever heard it. My memory of it is a school pal singing the chorus; she said it was the theme tune of a TV show starring a boy who had Down syndrome; she tried to be cute about it but I know it melted her heart to see a boy like her beloved little cousin on TV. And, you know what? I had forgotten about that cousin. I had even forgotten I ever had that friend until I heard that woman sing that song.

It is a sweet song. I thought of you anyway, even though you don't own a note of it, that I know of. The woman sounded bad, but she was brave. Feelings bloomed in me: fear, courage, love, pride, loss. *Are* these feelings? I walked them off. Saw a shawl-wearing woman in a doorway.

'Are you here for the supper?' she asked me. Maybe I'd been staring at her. I do that to people, as you know.

I bought a ticket for the supper and a raffle ticket that I might win a handmade blanket that was tacked to the wall inside. It wasn't to my taste. If I won the blanket I planned to give it to someone, if I got talking to anyone. The woman insisted that if I won she would post it home to me. The thought of going home soon was too sad, especially with that ugly blanket.

'Thank you,' I said.

I wonder how many times I had said those two words during those two months. Too, too many.

I took only a little supper, purely for show, then sat at a table with two women who had arrived together and had no interest in me. Another woman joined us.

'Are you a teacher?' she asked me.

'No,' I said.

She smiled and ate her rice.

I could think of nothing to say to her. There might have been thoughts going on in my head – like, why did she say that of all the things there were to say?

But I had spent so long being silent I could not pick thoughts out and hold them to the light. After she ate she went into another room. I mentioned the homemade blanket to the two women facing me. They were not as impressed as I feigned feeling about it.

'It *is* a women artists' supper,' one said with a shrug, as if I was missing something. Of course I was missing everything. I lifted the programme and scanned it, it had names and a scheduled speech. The name of the speaker appeared masculine.

I realised everyone was going to the next room for an art display and went to check it out. Of course some pieces were good and some were bad and some I think I *felt* ... and that's probably enough art talk for you. I know you're not one for it, so I won't go on. I know you think all art is pain.

I walked back into the supper room and sat down noticing a man in the supper queue. I wondered if he was there to make the speech. Interesting, I thought, that the speaker for a women's event should be a man, but I won't go on about that, I know my thoughts on gender grate on you.

He took a seat beside me. I was glad, I won't lie. I felt he wanted to talk. Just not to me. I knew he knew I was foreign. He could tell by my hair and my clothes, and by the way I stared at him. Which I never realised I did until you told me so. Maybe I should thank you for that?

I looked away and found my cup on the table.

'So,' he said, 'you are artists?' This question was aimed at the women facing me.

They watched him suspiciously, one of them nodded.

'How are you an artist?' he asked the one on our left.

'How? Textiles,' she said.

'And how are you an artist?' he asked the one on our right.

'Watercolours. Pastels too.'

The women looked unimpressed. I could tell he was not the speechmaker.

'And you?' he said to me although I knew he did not want to. 'You an artist?'

'No,' I said and took a drink. Turned out I did not want to talk.

The woman on our left stared at him. 'I suppose,' she said, 'this is where we ask you if you are an artist.'

'I work with soil,' he said, 'so I suppose you could say I am a truer artist than any of you.'

'So who are you, God?' She rolled her eyes. I envied her that eye roll, that remark, that she could embarrass a person like that, that she could know his plan all along. The women started to talk amongst themselves.

I knew the man must have been there for the visiting Australian lecturer's seminars. I had sat beside the lunchtime tables of geologists, recognising some from their photos, and had heard them talk about excursions, which I went on the next day alone. I suppose lunchtimes were when I could have said, 'Hey, I'm a geologist too, can I tag along?'

But I did not want to tag. I did not want to tell the man at my elbow, *hey, I work with soil too*. I did not want the women artists to roll their eyes at me, then see me like they saw him, there to feed on their pain work, even though I had just eaten very well already.

I went outside as night fell. Amateur hour was over in the square. A band played one of your songs. I could have sat down and listened but I walked into a bar instead.

'Hi there,' said the pretty server. 'In for food?'

'No. Drinks,' I said. 'Lots of them.'

'It's like that, is it!' She smiled and set down a beer mat. 'What will we be starting with?'

I looked at her name badge.

'You're called Emerson,' I said.

'Seems so.'

'That's my name too.' Yes, I know it sounds juvenile but I said it.

'No way!' she said. 'Well, Emerson, what can I get you?'

Nights when there was entertainment going on in the square the bar stayed empty, so she joined me for some drinks and my first conversation in almost months.

By the end of the night she walked me home. Details escape me but I know I couldn't find my key card.

'Not trying to molest you, Emerson,' she said rummaging through my jean pockets.

'Oh, you can if you like,' I said.

I'm sorry. Is that too much information?

When I woke up the next morning her head was on the pillow beside mine, she was staring at me when I opened my eyes. I stared back and she smiled.

'Emerson,' she said. 'Anyone ever tell you you're stinking cute when you sleep?'

'Yes,' I said. 'One person.'

Of course I wasn't talking about you.

PROVISION

THE RAIN, LIKE chaos, hits the window and glides down and over the ledge, onto the grey soil of the lot, turning it fresh and black as ink. Parker taps his pen on his desk to the beat of rainwater that drums in an old paint pot sitting by his feet. The skylight has let in buckets of the stuff, which keeps bringing old chips of paint back to life. Out of the window, the cattle step through sweet clover that is already flattened by the sweet-smelling rain. Having always known the importance of letters, Parker drafts one for the local paper; having to share his opinion, which often derails halfway through each letter's composition. As long as he is passionate about a cause at the time Parker is writing, and he is, this is good enough for him. This time there is no changing of minds.

    He wonders where the children from the photos are now, as he stands on the polished floor of his study in stockinged feet, feeding old, wrung-out newspapers to the fire. Then Parker sits and makes three small edits before typing up his letter to post it the next day. First he must carry his small, sleeping daughter out of her bed and into his truck, and go collect Sarah and her tables and their silverware.

We have water in the house, Parker tells Mike the next morning as they take a pew in Starbucks.

    They are each clutching a bottle of newly-bought soda, and Parker is wearing his Sunday best; he is looking out at the deserted and rain-beaten street at the shiny copper statue of an ex-president who lurks permanently patriotic on the corner of the street. Downtown, there is one on every corner.

    We have just over six inches at our house, Mike says. He is wearing a baseball cap and shorts. He takes a drink.

    You can see from the bypass, when you're driving by, Parker says. And more water at the top of our lot line. We're a little worried about it. Looks like the sun might come out.

You think? says Mike. He examines his bottle. Three dollars for this, he says, did I hear her right?

Parker smiles. So, what else is new? You went for that interview?

I went to the interview, says Mike getting comfortable. It was weird; I got the letter and it said: Dress code: Wear what you like.

That is weird, Parker says.

Yeah, so you know me, says Mike. I had to know what that meant. They always say wear what you like, but really …

Yeah, Parker agrees.

So, I went.

You did? How did it go?

Firstly, says Mike rolling his wrists, I emailed and asked what to wear; and they got back to me and were like: Really … wear what you like.

Hmm.

So, I got there and mostly people were wearing suits.

Really? Damn. Parker shakes his head, tightening, untightening the lid of his soda bottle.

Then there was this one dude, says Mike, and he was wearing cargo shorts. It was just weird, you know. And then, um, there's ten of us. So, like …

That's quite a lot.

Yeah, says Mike. And I'm not paranoid but I'm like, sceptical or whatever, but I thought, one of these guys is a plant.

Oh, like not really there for the interview? asks Parker.

Right. I had it narrowed down to the dude in the cargo pants, or this dude who was like a nervous copper. He never stopped talking. But it was good. It put people at ease. Even still, I'm a conspiracy theorist, says Mike. So, I do my test, which was strange too, because the questions were not what I thought they'd be.

There are photos of people, he continues, just all different kinds of people, and you have to write, plus three to negative three, how much you are sexually attracted to someone. Guys, girls, old people …

I'd give everyone negative three, says Parker. I think that's what you should have done. Or maybe they'd be expecting you to score a certain way and I'd hit it up at random: say, a negative two here, and a one, a positive two here …

Yeah, but, says Mike

Unless it's your wife, Parker puts in.

Yes, Mike says. But they had, say, a teenage girl who is dressed a little older; I mean, like, do you be honest?

That's crazy.

Yes, crazy, seriously.

You should get paid a tonne of money for it, says Parker.

It was voluntary, I had to pay to go there, says Mike. So then … you take the chance, you do that, then I had to go in and the interviewer asks – first question: Why are you wearing that? And then he says: Oh, you're the guy who emailed.

Crazy! says Parker.

Second question, says Mike, how long have I kept you waiting? I knew it was twenty minutes. And third question: How many applicants are there altogether. I said to the interviewer: Well, initially you said nine. You're the only person who picked up on that, he told me. So, I go in for the second interview and who's there on the panel?

The guy in the cargo pants? asks Parker.

No. The nervous copper.

That's hilarious, that's hilarious.

They are constantly testing your observation skills, says Mike. It was good, it was intense though. When I got done at the end of the day I was exhausted.

Yes, it's the rigours of being in a situation.

Right, right, says Mike. It's overwhelming.

Are you still convinced that you would like it?

Oh yeah. I would.

That's great, it really is.

They said I should hear something in like two weeks.

Great, says Parker, I wish you well with it.

They sit quietly for a while, then Parker says: You know, I don't know anymore, it feels like we are living under some regime.

Mike frowns.

I mean, I speak to God, says Parker, and he is listening and I just don't know. I want so much to be that good man.

Yeah, right, right, says Mike looking around at a woman who has been typing non-stop in the corner and has not touched her iced coffee. There is a bite taken out of her glowing white apple. She could be a distraction but she is not.

They take those little kids from their parents, says Parker.

That's what you mean by a regime. Mike laughs dryly.

They are looking for asylum, says Parker. I don't think they are criminals.

Right, you don't. Uh-huh. Mike takes another drink. It does look like the sun is coming out, he says.

That will be nice, maybe I'll get out for a hike.

I'm renting a house in Keystone.

You are? asks Parker.

Oh, yeah. So, I can take all day, don't have to go to bed by a certain time, can sleep late. I can nap during the day.

That's pretty nice.

Go for hikes, says Mike.

Nice.

You and Sarah should join Karel and me at the weekend.

I'd love to, says Parker.

It's on Playhouse Road.

Dude, oh my gosh, really?

It's something.

Gosh, Mike dude, says Parker, his throat closing. My eyes start to water when you say something that is already overwhelming to me.

Mike smiles with his eyes squinted small.

But I'll have to check, Parker says. Sarah is working weekends. She had to do a wedding at Nemo last night. It was an outdoor thing. We cleaned up, took away the tables and our silverware. We weren't getting home till 2 a.m.

Can't you leave your tables and you can get them in the morning? asks Mike.

Not really, says Parker. She had two weddings booked this month. And next month … two July weddings.

Okay.

She can't carry the stuff by herself. It's my truck, I don't want Little Bill driving my truck. All her stuff. I told her maybe she could hire help and give them twelve dollars an hour.

Right. Mike takes another sip and looks out of the window.

Parker extends on his point: I'm making money, she says, and I'm like, Jesus, stop. We have a daughter and you need to stay home for that daughter. But she's like: I have a business, it's a small business, but it does make money.

I read a quote by CS Lewis lately, says Mike sharply, always impatient with prattle – Lewis is saying that the homemaker is the ultimate profession; that all other professions exist to support it.

Parker laughs. Oh, man, he says.

I better get going, says Mike. I'll let you know … about that hike.

Once Mike leaves, Parker stays to use the restroom, then he sits down again and lifts the local paper from which he reads some more about the detainees held at the border.

In the photo that accompanies the piece are the little children, they are lying on some floor and wrapped in foil like oven-ready chicken parcels. Then, over the page, another article, this time about the postal service; it states that there has been a recent surge of people sending letters to God, and being that there is nowhere to put them, the letters are going to be burned.

On the way home, Parker watches from his truck as his congregation is swallowed by the church doors and a thought pops into his head, or a voice, that says: Go home and pray in your closet.

At home, he does exactly that, between mothballed shirts and Christmas pullovers. Then he joins Sarah and their daughter for Sunday lunch.

Sarah is dishing out steak and potatoes; she is in a pleated skirt, she smells of cinnamon. Quietly she is listening as Parker tells her about the new letter he wrote for the paper, about the detained children he has read about in the media.

Downtown there is this sign, she says sitting down to eat, it's everywhere actually.

Which sign? he asks.

It's a hotline, a couple of dollars a minute. People call it and they ask for answers for things they'd prefer not to waste their time mulling over.

That's ridiculous, says Parker.

Is it?

It is, I think.

Hmm, I don't know, says Sarah, slipping a heel in and out of her pump. It's possibly better than the Rightful Timescale.

The Rightful? I'm not sure I know what you're talking about.

Yeah, she says, it's when you give yourself a certain time limit to consider a thing. So, like, say I am wondering what to make for dinner …

Right.

I'd think, what have I got in the fridge? Do I go tuna? Or pasta? Do I go and get something else? Parker, people can waste hours thinking about stuff like that.

They do?

I know I do, says Sarah.

Hours? he asks.

Maybe one hour, split up throughout the day.

Parker eats his lunch with new consideration.

Whereby, say you have a bigger decision to make.

Like to employ staff to help you with your tables? he asks.

That will do, says Sarah. So, is that medium or large? That's probably large.

In your case, one staff member, two hours a night, twice a month. Medium?

Say it's medium; so, ten minutes is all the consideration that question needs.

Speaking of, says Parker, I don't want Little Bill driving my truck and I don't want someone who doesn't care about your supplies bashing everything about. And someone needs to be home with our daughter.

Right, of course, Sarah says. We're going off topic. So, large dilemmas are, like: should I relocate? invest? and so on.

How long do large dilemmas get, on the Rightful Timescale?

Sarah shrugs. Coupla hours.

Getting back … what is the helpline for? asks Parker.

Okay. Sarah eats some mashed potato. You phone them up and they just cut out the middle person, and the wasted time; they tell you what you should do. Immediately.

Like, they give you bad financial advice?

No, I don't think it's like that.

Sounds like a scam.

It just lights a little fire under you, says Sarah.

People use this service?

I know they do.

Who do you know? asks Parker.

Lots of people … take Mike and Karel.

Stop it. Mike and Karel?

They've used it when they've wanted to make career decisions.

Mike didn't mention that.

Maybe he is embarrassed. It's a peculiar thing, admittedly.

Peculiar, yes, says Parker.

I just think that sometimes people shy away from decisions. They want someone to focus them, to listen to them, you know.

Yes, I do.

The rain has stopped but the study's skylight still leaks. Parker scans a copy of the latest paper to find that his letter has not been published again. The usual float of disappointment wells up inside him, up to chest-level, just behind his nipples.

The letters that have made it into the paper are nothing new. They are about the local uranium mines, and the old unforgotten flood, and other tragedies that people care to have remembered.

Not often, not today, but sometimes, there are letters complimenting the manners of young people, or thanking someone for a kind gesture, but Parker cannot remember the last time he read this type of correspondence. Working back from the letters page, he finds a development on a story he has been following, about a father on trial for the murder of his nineteen-month-old daughter. The initial story, as Parker remembers, was non-suspicious; the child's mother stated that the little girl fell in the bath, and fell down some steps. Now they're saying that the child's father is expected to blame the child's mother because, as a minor, she once committed a felony, but that file is sealed. Parker reads that there will be a decision made soon as to whether that old file will be opened and all the details brought to light, which just seems wrong to him. All of it, every edge of the story, seems sharp to Parker.

The child's face still sticks in his mind. And in her face, he sees the other face he now knows so well; the face of the little girl detainee who cries permanently at the back of his eyes, as she has her shoelaces tied by her mother for the last time in God knows how long, just before they are pulled away from each other; which there is no photo for, just a narrative, but it is the image Parker pictures most when he pictures the little girl. When he pictures any little girl. Even his own.

By now his letter seems like nothing, by now he is embarrassed about it. Parker goes to the post office and opens a PO Box.

The next week he receives a message to tell him that the box is full, that he needs to come and collect.

And there are hundreds of letters in there already, they are mostly addressed simply to God. Some to God in Heaven, a few to My Sweet Lord. Parker brings them home in his truck and spreads them over the dining table.

Where did you get this idea? asks Sarah. Was it because of the hotline?

No, he says. This will not generate an income.

Nor should it, she says, but how interesting. Sarah lifts a fan of letters then she fetches a butter knife from the drawer.

We can't open them, Parker says. Can you imagine what is in there, what would happen if we were to read them?

I have little interest in reading them, says Sarah. I can equally leave them alone.

The week after, with word gotten out, there are close to a thousand letters for Parker to collect. Which he boxes and stacks in his study. When he has a moment, he spends it looking at the boxes with his eyes full of tear-water.

I was thinking about hotlines, says Sarah joining him with their red-cheeked daughter on her hip. You know those hotlines you get – she covers their daughter's open ear – whereby children can speak to Father Christmas?

Vaguely, he says, folding in the top of the highest box.

You know it's automated, right?

It is?

Yes, she says. Father C goes: What would you like? have you been good? and then he says: That's great! before you have a chance to answer.

I don't remember, admits Parker.

Oh, I do, says Sarah. I called one once, I was probably in the second grade.

There is another money generator, he says, if that's what you're thinking. Like the decision-making one.

I don't want business ideas.

You're right. It's just not ethical.

No, Sarah says. It's not *not* ethical. As long as the charge isn't too much, and children get something from it …

Out of the window the soil is finally lightening in colour and drying out. The cattle are roaming, and the air is humid and sweet.

You'd need a longer pause, says Parker, or else it gives the game away. Or, not automate it but actually listen. Actually reply.

Sure, she says. But we're busy with the ranch, and the baby, and that's not why I'm telling you this.

Hey, Sarah, he says, wouldn't it be good to work from home? You could be with our daughter. Little Bill would do a great Father Christmas impersonation, and the idea would still be yours.

Parker! I have a business, she says. It's a small business, but it does make money.

He tickles his daughter's foot. She pulls away and laughs.

You know CS Lewis? Parker asks Sarah.

Of Narnia?

Yes, he says. Lewis had a saying about a homemaker, about the homemaker being the best career path there is.

Sarah sighs. He's gone a long time. And it's not his homemaking talents anyone's talking about.

It's not about notoriety, says Parker.

Isn't it? Then, I wonder, can you talk a little about why you write to the newspaper? Sarah asks.

I just have something to say. Like, an opinion.

You never sign off anonymously.

Since starting up the PO Box I haven't written a single letter, says Parker.

You like best when someone responds to your letter, Sarah says, positive or negative, you're happy.

Parker studies her.

People aren't as ignorant as you seem to think, she says, they know their god is not getting these letters. They know it is a person. A humble, good person.

How do they know the person is good?

Like a bad person will do this? Most people shut out cruelty. But not you. You, Parker, are exactly the kind of person who can give people hope.

Parker only once relents and opens a letter, then stuffs it back into the envelope before he can see the sender's name and in doing so release some curse like a black moth. He thinks about the detained children, who are still not with their families, and about the protests made from the outrage of good ordinary people who believe they can make a small change in the world.

He thinks about the actions of the people who detained those children. They would, Parker thinks, like to learn of more ways in which they can further hurt people, especially those who need help, whose faith in being listened to is diminishing. This in mind, he goes to his closet.

Dear whomever or whichever force that deals with such things, he says, see that I have adequate strength to get me through this. Or tell me, what should I do? Should I stop writing letters to the paper?

No, comes a reply. You should not.

Should not what? he asks. Should not stop?

Parker waits but the reply does not arrive.

Should I advise that people need to stop writing to you, Lord?

Yes, is the reply.

You are disappointed in me, whispers Parker, his nose is stuck in the collar of a mothballed shirt; he is a hair closer to moral clarity. And I should close the PO Box? he adds to another wait, and this time, no reply.

On a Saturday evening, before he collects Sarah, their silverware and her tables from somebody else's happiest day, Parker fills up his truck with boxes full of letters for God.

He drives his young daughter to a campsite, where, as he fashions a pit fire, Parker remembers how he once found a postal worker at his screen door, clutching a letter he was meant to be delivering. One summer, the man just appeared there, staring intently at the envelope. Parker had coughed to get his attention.

Oh. Got some post for you, the postal worker said, pinking up. I think it's a job application, so I was casting a little good luck over it for ya.

Disbelieving and dubious then, Parker now identifies and appreciates the compliment, as he holds each letter for a moment, as if trying to dissolve it into a prayer, then lets the envelope fall and go up in smoke.

He waits for the flames to give out, checking in every so often on his daughter, whom he can see is still sleeping through the sparkling window of his truck. He cannot leave even one God Letter intact or in a recognisable state, Parker thinks, as he assesses the scene at his feet. Down on hands and knees, with a flashlight in his mouth and a zippo in his hand, Parker individually relights every larger shred until all that is left is ash, absolute.

He finishes up just in time when the rain restarts, the bouncing hail of it waking his daughter, who is now upright in her car seat, and watching out of the window with eyes that look like deep dark hollows in this light. From this space.

She smiles, her eyes wet from the cry her father hasn't heard. She is smiling for that father, who is running towards her and his truck, dodging a new wave of rain, and looking just like a flame dancing on the rapidly darkening earth.

OTHER CHILDREN

Sweater, noun: garment worn by child when its mother is feeling chilly.
– Ambrose Bierce

IT WAS IN the final decade of Marin Kinsey's life when she found herself in a rich collision with madness. The morning it began, she had crashed her head off the kitchen wall. Marin had been awake an hour already, she was feeding her son breakfast when he became antsier than usual.

Marin knew that his diaper was clean, she had just seen to that; but for a reason she would never know, Cal turned and searched for the wall with those long fingers she imagined, in some parallel realm, running to earth over Stravinsky's *Firebird*, leaving buttery comet tails on the mimosa-coloured paint; and then, with quick consideration, he lurched his head against the plaster.

Marin tried to pull him back but at ten years old Cal was strong, long, lean, slim-muscled as a rabbit, so she placed her hand between his head and the wall instead. She thought of the quip Calder Sr. had made in bed a few hours earlier. She had said: Is he banging his head off the cot? And Calder's response had been swallowed up by his pillow. He wouldn't do it if it hurt. Or something like that.

Once Cal stopped wrestling against her, in both interest and impulse, Marin cracked her own skull.

It was standing in their narrow, truncated kitchen with a bushfire of crazy at one side of her head that she had what some would call an epiphany: there had to be some constituency of people who could placate this pain and stop her crumbling into mental breakdown.

At 6 a.m., when Calder eventually got up, he elaborated that what he had meant was that their son must have found some angle at which cot bars, or indeed kitchen walls, did not fully impact.

He suggested she have a cigarette while he led Cal to his safe zone: a pillow-strewn therapy space once intended as a bedroom for other children; other children who never materialised in that home. Marin stood outside looking into the old kitchen that far outkitchened friendships, marriages, even lives, now you think of it.

Outside, the maple tree sounded its silent siren against a breeze of light and dark; making it September. Making the year 1991. The air was not warm, more electric, clove-stung. Oysterish almost, and the plane for California headed over their Boston home like it always did at that time. Marin inhaled her daily smoke with the same feeling she had had for the last nine or so years already; that it would be healthy to want to be onboard, going somewhere; that every thought that was surely healthy was leaving her.

As soon as the school bus came for Cal that morning, a full wearing day already behind them, Calder left for his office and Marin went off on the hunt for a support group even though, as a rule, she had no predilection for people when they came grouped, and she never cared to talk about her son, especially not to strangers, whom everyone was to Marin, in reality, apart from Cal.

The group she located was aswarm with women. In the beginning they liked to judge one another. Yet over the years Marin contrived to commit until the group evolved into an embassy of inclusion: women she could almost confide in, who not only sought support but offered it.

☺

One night, a year or so later, with Calder snoring bedside her, and Marin fresh home from the weekly whirring insomnia of a group exchange that was always intensified by the silver coffee urn, she thought about Lily Place: a mother from the support group.

Marin could not get Lily's story out of her mind, nor could she keep it scalpel-free.

Lily had told the rest of the MOMs – Mothers Over Minds, they called themselves – how she remembered being out for lunch in a café facilitated by 'handicapped' people, when her husband – what had his name been? had Lily mentioned it? – had made a cruel joke at a worker's expense. Lily likes to say that this was the first strand of her doubt, and being a person to never forget a slight – on anyone's behalf – when the Places had a daughter born with Down syndrome, Lily knew she must tell her husband their marriage was done. And then, after telling the MOMs this, Lily lifted her coffee cup, sat back and smiled. To Marin this fact was the most salient part, the getting rid of the experience through the telling of it.

There was also Naomi Leap: a MOM who renovated what it meant to care for and yet seem carefree. Indomitable, relaxed and never run aground; Naomi was not wrapped in the same thin membrane of social mistrust that encased Marin. She had other children, not just the boy with MS, who was her primary reason for attending the support group, she also had one either side: the older child who was *a great help*, and the youngest, who was a sweet kid with Asperger's, with whom Marin was particularly taken.

Naomi's mind, it seemed, could ping right back into shape but Marin knew that her life would be easier, better, fuller, if Cal had not lifted that germy toy, like all kids do, and put it to his mouth.

Cal ate dirt while Marin stirred the sweetness out of her coffee.

His brain inflamed like a balloon while she checked a receipt for an intuited discrepancy.

They had brought him home and had to learn the new Cal, learning impaired; them learning that his world was now sensory and yet he had lost two. Lost his senses. Lost.

That elastic moment eclipsed her.

Why me? she would ask herself. Why Cal?

That should have been the question. This was correct; it was not happening to her.

Not directly.

Marin had her senses. Her life was a demonstration of sense. She had her carefree childhood and everything ordinary. Everything that Cal deserved to have. But sometimes he was so ill that he could not go to school, and so Marin could not hold a job, reframing her dreams within the vectors of four walls, while Cal – was he even aware, she wondered – when in a good health spell, would live a more outdoorsy life than his mother, with a much better social life.

☺

Over the years most of the parents in the group split up, as did Marin and Calder Jackman, despite their give and take hobble, and Marin's fear of ministering to Cal solo, and that financial squeeze on them both. Three people on one person's salary! They had scraped it together, always had wine and smokes. Marin was never permitted to put her teaching degree to use, with Cal being the honeymoon baby to college graduates. She had even soured on giving piano lessons. These factors swamped them. Stress was the milquetoast cousin of this new feeling, and this new feeling was sorrow.

Calder took Cal weekends until he found someone new, as Marin had expected him to do, as was par for the course with the other halves of MOMs. Calder and his new partner, Ava, gave Cal a little brother called Emile. Emile could talk and be funny, with intention and without it, and Calder showed up at his old home considerably less often. He found that he could no longer do Sundays; not that there is anything holy about Sundays, just that they are good family days for second families. Marin, if she were not numb, would have respected him for trying over.

☺

On her own for eight years, Marin met JB Levin, who was radiant and good, and despite her commitments – as MOMs like Lily and Naomi liked to remind her – he stepped into the theatre of risk and did not bail.

He got nice recognition for this, making Marin sense that she was not radiant nor good enough for JB, nor, she suspected, for any man with half of his traits.

JB would call in the evening and sit with her and Cal, and she would understand most solidly that she was not the best girlfriend that JB could have, nor that she could be. Her home had the indelible, churlish stings of public urinals and medicinal liniments, and her best years had been spent up the same way they still were, the way they were till her dying day.

JB would not sleep over; JB would go home, and Cal would go to bed and cry, banging his head against the cot. And in her room Marin would cry too, her tears putting a halo on the desk light burning on the landing, she would pull the loose cuticle of bedding back over her feet until Cal would stop whimpering and the night would return to dark noises: gassy floorboards, glassy electricity, and she would not get out of bed to see what had misfired. And in the morning, during the soft unruliness of his sleep, Cal's diaper had either worked off or he had shredded it into sparkling wet cumin-yellow crystals, or his faeces was smeared to the bars of the cot and dried in, and Marin would cry again until she felt better for doing so.

She did not want to share this with JB, she could not bear the thought of sharing these classified matters – her son's human comedy – nor that Cal would bounce on his commode within the refitted shower, the water running a muddy lake off his groin as Marin abolished the umber flakes from his arms with a towel dried outdoors for its scouring proficiency.

No, she could not tell him these particulars. Instead she took this step, when JB called around, to exhale, soften her shoulders, and Marin would say, only inside herself, it is okay and it will be okay, JB is not going to leave me. He can do better, but he doesn't see it today.

She would become funny and calm, and set about approving of herself when he was there. And JB was nice enough to act as though he was fooled, often telling Marin that she was a saint, and again she would feel run aground.

Though sometimes she would lift the lid on the old baby grand instead and play a tune neither carefully nor heavily.

☺

Marin took the outfit Cal had worn to the facility's end of year dance and headed for his room before the alarm had the chance to sound. It was two minutes prior to 5 a.m., early-mid-September light was spraying onto his face. Cal hadn't worn a tuxedo to the dance like some of the boys because, heart and soul that would have finished Marin off. Instead she had purchased a beautiful, full-price cashmere sweater and a dribble bib that resembled a cravat. At the dance the other MOMs had joked around, acting like the kids were regular teens.

No sneaking rum into the punch bowl when you think we aren't looking, Naomi Leap said.

Don't think we don't know what kids get up to at school dances! said Lily Place.

Marin wore her stock smile, adding a few soundbites to show she did not think that the whole entire scene was the most hope-hammering thing she had ever witnessed: the Place girl with the striking Barbie doll figure and a sweet face marked with Down's, glitter on her shoulders, a pink corsage on her wrist; and the Leaps' austerely thin boy in the red-wheeled battery-powered chair, his hair gelled slick, a black satin bow tie arranged undone on his bridge of a collar bone as he slept through the excitement; and Cal. Cal? Marin knew her Cal was different: Calder Jackman Jr., a name destined for an office door, aircraft pilot, Ministry of Defense.

Cal used to walk, used to climb into her lap and press his nose against hers until they went out of each other's focus; and before he had language, before he had language to lose, his chubby fingers would point to show that he needed her. He had seen her with roving curiosity, and heard her voice. Then Cal's default setting had two gears, and yet he was not cross-wired from the start.

The night of the dance Marin could barely look at him. There wasn't a day she wasn't thinking what he would do when she was gone.

☺

Behind closed blinds the maple tree shook like steam. Marin took the electric shaver and ran it over his cheeks and chin. She brushed his teeth and kissed his forehead to the same giggle she had come to expect unless Cal was sick. She brushed his beautiful, straight, white teeth that she didn't see a lot of at the facility then she lifted her suitcase and steered Cal outside into the car, returning to zip the house up.

It would have been the right thing, in many people's opinions, to go to the Jackman house and tell Calder this was how it was going to be. That it was fate. Well, it seemed to be, although what fate is exactly is too big a question, and the returns were not yet in, and so she drove.

☺

Because there were families at the airport, Marin felt disconcerted. And it was Tuesday. Not that she was naming days, just numbering them, like magpies.

Day one, Marin thought, September 11th, regarding JB as he lifted a tray, asking what she would like for breakfast. Marin told him to pick something for himself of which she would have a little, and JB smiled a smile that was proportionately fond and bruised: a smile that could mean a whole marshalling of things.

For this complexity – this different complexity – she was indebted.

They sat huddled at a table, Marin listening to the everyday demands of parents to other children. They were so demanding; they did not communicate with each other outside of instructions. Some mornings she would sit in a café and drink her cappuccino and just listen to mothers bray directives at their toddlers:

Sit up! Get down! *Get down on the floor!* Don't snatch! all this while looking exasperated as if they had it so hard.

Or; Behave this instant, that woman is looking over, some mother would say as she tried to keep all at her table picture perfect and quiet. Marin would look around herself to find that she was *that woman*, and she would feel an inexplicable slice of pride because she and Cal asked nothing of each other.

He relied on her and she, tired and by rote, obliged, and he, most of the time, would giggle, and she would feel probably happier than these breakfast moms felt about their kids. This other life, the life everyone else seemed to have, non-MOMs, looked profound and animated, it looked like disappointment with tiny blips of joy. The success other children needed to acquire would surely have to be epic for their mothers to feel half of Marin's joy. And there was joy with Cal. There undoubtedly was.

At the table next to theirs was a father, he was telling the little girl that she could open her juice box herself, telling her there was no such word as can't. Marin remembered how she used to tell her students the same back in teaching college; she always said it but she was never convinced. And yet there was Cal, and he could not. Why was that so sorrowful, the can't? The could not? To be unable to move forward? Why? Why her? But really, why him?

Every time Cal's face came into Marin's mind, she pushed him back, covered him with a layer of some novelty, let the pedals of her heart spin. She ignored that opaque spot inside it, following solely the ecstasy and exhilaration of being foreign in an airport with JB.

They headed through to security, which was never part of what she pictured when she thought about taking this trip to his hometown – if a trip is what we call adventures that must come to an end.

If you're ever in Cali I'll show you the sights, he'd said.

JB had suggested this fortnight away from two decades of responsibilities. And okay: that suited her. The doubt comes later. If it comes at all.

That morning in the airport lobby she stood by the payphone for a moment almost calling home. Like Cal was even there, and even if he was, like he could answer.

She was doing what she wanted, wasn't she? This was what she had craved: a little brain freeze: some time to do what other people get to, even the other MOMs, occasionally; and Calder, most of the time.

Marin held the receiver with a gut-tug that made her contemplate phoning Calder, but she hated to hear Emile in the background. He always answered, even if she called when he should be at school, Emile would be home for the day, rocking a hard-thought migraine or a sprained wrist from a skateboarding mishap, and just on cue, and in a shining voice, he would have to ask his mother or father for something – the way children with normative development seem to – when they were otherwise engaged in Cal-talk with Marin. So she hung up, her hands woody and dusty, feeling like a stranger to herself. They were leaving soon.

☺

Long before, Marin had reconciled herself with the thought of losing her freedom because it was the only choice. Then she had a dream.

For the first time in her life it was not about Calder, nor one were you wind up naked at school or at work. Marin had work, and Cal was it; an unrecognised workstation and the hardest job she knew of, and Marin was always exhausted because of it.

If she was alternately fortunate, or unfortunate, enough to wake in the midst of a dream, she would learn why she was so damn tired in the mornings, for even her nights were spent pushing, fighting for her son's life, and his rights, while she only found sleep in showers. Even in her dreams she was listening for the diaper rustle. Cal could manage to tussle himself Houdini-like out of all-in-one suits that were zipped at the back and had the neck adjusted, the feet cut out.

She would dress him in it, this man; grown, and taller than her, heavier, too.

She had had this dream. She and Cal had been to the woods, like she used to bring him when she could still manage his chair over the terrain.

She had poured leaves over his face and he had laughed and been peaceful, and then, even second-guessing her dream, thinking to herself, We are both going to stay here, to sleep, maybe even die here.

Marin remembered it exactly because it woke her, and came back to her, not during the days when what she knew best, when caring, took over the job of escaping, but at night; Marin would put her head on the lumpy brain of her pillow and *bam!* it was back, the vision of her and her son both sleeping under the trees, her holding his hand, and then, that scene which always stirred her awake: the part when she stood up, dusted herself down, looked at Cal and told him – like every morning – that she loved him deeply, and saw his face at peace as she crept away.

But Calder said that no way he could manage a fortnight, he would be gone with work and it was unfair to ask Ava to manage Cal alone; and Marin knew that neither could he, because Cal's father had allowed himself to forget how, only taking an overnight here and there, sleeping in the room with Cal so as to catch him before he would smear poop, or to hush his cries before he woke Ava and Emile.

So Marin told Calder, Forget it! Knowing which buttons to push to keep him away. You were always a lousy father, and obviously love Emile the most; JB will take better care of me, the three of us will go to California together, she said.

Which was an ordinary boast to relieve Calder some of that heavy-duty guilt he was sitting on, and to have him disappointed in her, and on a deeper level himself, while simultaneously overriding it with the gift of relief that there was always someone else for him to handover to.

But, in fairness, she had sprung it on him. The night before the trip was short notice; and a bottle of wine conversation, if they could still do that.

But they had chosen to split, unknowingly choosing to be unobtainable to each other from then on.

There must have been a choice Marin didn't remember making. There must always be a choice. You can always walk away, although you'd never think it.

She made the choice to tell JB that Cal had gone to his father's.

Before JB came to take her to the airport, Marin took Cal out early. She opened Cal's car door and stood behind him, his weight top-heavy leaning back against her, his torso tight and knot-free, hair all wildflower, his wire-tight body clock sensing that it was desperately early to be out and about, and that the air was different.

She guided him through the forest, her back twinging. They passed a lake where water had lathered itself into a plastic foam. Leaves had made a wreath along the edge where water and land met. They walked for half an hour more, finding a space where Marin could lay out the picnic blanket.

She got Cal, her arms shaking, she lowered him to the ground, accidentally making him bump his head and burst into ill-timed giggles. Marin stood over him and finally exhaled.

Cal joined his hands together and brought them to his chin, like a prayer, almost; she saw him chew the insides of his mouth, his face filled with pale Boston morning light. Cal coughed about the rattling silverware of his lungs. Marin looked up, made sure the trees would shade him from the sun, if it got too much.

Then she lay down. Watched weeds nibble at the grass. She heard fear as a passenger.

Marin took a baggy from her purse and a wet wipe to clean his face again then Cal began to cry. She sat up, tried to soothe him by stroking his hand.

It's okay, she said.

He cried some more.

Get down on the floor!

He cried sobs like water dripping into a porcelain sink. Milky and clean.

Tears were good, she thought, they were needed sometimes, to calm a body, to chase away bad energy. Tears were as good for poor vision as they were for nervous souls.

Get down on the floor!

Marin Kinsey lay back again.

She tried to hug him; she did this to suggest that this was also *not* what she wanted. She slipped her fingers over Cal's face, the smooth ridge of his nose, around the soft apples of his cheeks, there were no missed patches of facial hair, like over his lip.

JB had taught her how to do it properly, joking that women don't know about guy stuff. He always had *the guy talk* with Cal. She imagined that Cal could smell this other smell, feel JB's hand of reassurance on his shoulder as he took over, coming to the rescue to shave Marin's son's face.

Cal's hands would release from the anxious prayer-like way in which he would grip them when his mother shaved him, anticipating a nick here and there.

Cal preferred JB, she thought. Maybe he did. Maybe in seeped a brotherhood with no requisite for words or visuals, just an innate understanding that someone was a good person and will understand, or at least have empathy, if compassion is too much to ask for, when all is said and done.

FEAR

FOR A WHILE I was one of those women I used to like the look of: the kind who walks into a restaurant to meet someone, and on seeing that someone gathers her skirts and canters over, then wraps the friend up in the most eloquent of hugs. For a while I was even this kind: the kind of woman who sees a farmer working in a field, and gives him a salute as she saunters on, rounding corners she does not know. For spells I think I may even have been both. I think I learned how to be them from watching others; I'm sure their mannerisms came from characters I'd read about in books. Eventually I tired of trying to be someone else because underneath I was always this one small thing: a girl, stuck at ten years old, still afeared of strange noises and the dark.

Oh, you often ask yourself if it's really as good for you as they say it is, this painting of the self-portrait. But you know deep down it would be easier to stay at home and deal with life as it unfolds, and not have to look at yourself face on.

I don't know if painting a self-portrait *is* good for you but I know it can be bad; hey, you can kid yourself for a while that it is not, like when I worked as a painter – in between getting back into it and giving it up again – back when Gill offered me his cottage to stay in and work.

Back then I was afeared to take that journey but life told me I needed the break, so for months I made myself look forward to going. With the stresses of life heavy on my shoulders, the thought of going to this cottage with my paints helped lift the weight off, split it in two. I hunkered down for an eight-hour trip, which I thought I would hate but I didn't since I had Mina for company.

Mina was and still is an artist, and she was our driver. We loaded her Land Rover with her crap and with mine and set off along the motorways.

Once we got going it didn't seem all that bad.

I had pictured us stopping somewhere nice for lunch or even at a petrol station but Mina produced salmon sandwiches from her bag which we ate as she drove, trying to get there before the light fell, which was before 5 p.m. at that time.

Have I mentioned that it was November? We had planned to share the cottage; the idea had come to me when I told her about Gill's cottage on the cliff, right where the land ran out, and Mina said that she would love to come too. We could work in the day, drink wine by night, take drives and go to a nice seafood restaurant that Gill – my old art college friend – had told me about. I checked with him and he said that it would be fine if Mina came too because we were both artists, Mina working in textiles and me with paints.

When we arrived, I said: How could anyone properly *live* here year-round?

It doesn't look as if they do, Mina said, though it would be a different place in the summer alright.

And I looked about me and had to agree as the sun set and a chill pierced straight through me.

I have gone through stages in my life when I have not liked to be alone, like before Alasdair came and left and I had no choice. I had no choice but to be alone when, on the second night at the cottage, Mina received a quiet crisis call from home and had to leave, leaving me carless and all alone in the cottage on the cliff by the ocean, and in a constant state of rehydration, and with the gales talking in mechanical voices to me as I tried to sleep in the loft. Then I remembered how much I hated to be on my own.

Mina left a bale of briquettes and kindling and although I had never lit a fire in my almost-forty years, I set myself the task, trying to dip into my mobile data on my second lonely night to research on YouTube how it might be done.

But the first night without her I could not fathom it and I went cold and without a colourful thing to watch for two days, until I found some firelighters under the sink.

Then, full of pride that I had done it, I sent Alasdair a photo. *Tada, I lit my first fire* – this was the accompanying text and he sent me back the thumbs up emoji. He was working all the time, and although he'd said that maybe I should have returned home when Mina did, because he could hear the uncertainty in my voice, I said no to him because I had spoken to myself and to myself had said: You are here to work and work you will. Then after a day or two days on my own it changed, and I told myself: You are here not to survive but to thrive, and I tried.

I saw the pub lights on and I walked downhill on my first lonely night and spoke to the barman. It was just me and him. He broke into the language of the place as he spoke and I did not understand him fully, or, at times, at all.

I had two glasses of wine while he told me about the seasons there, and about dead season, which was what he termed the time we were living in. He told me that the seafood restaurant therefore was closed, as was every restaurant for miles around, and he told me how he did not have to work in dead season either but he had fancied opening the pub that night, and so he had.

True enough, that was the one and only time during my stay I saw a bit of life buzzing down there at the bottom of the hill. City slicker, the barman called me and I realised I probably was, although I have been mainly suburban since the age of thirty, I had spent my life up until then living in big cities all round the world and thinking I had seen it all.

That night, over my wine, I sat by the pub fire and read my book, and by the time I stood to use the bathroom my legs were like jelly. The barman sighed after a couple of hours of me reading and drinking not so much and he asked if I'd like a lift back to the cottage, and I said: No, it's fine, then I realised that there was real and true tiredness in his eyes and I said that I would go. I was walking away when he called me back with a brusque tone, his lips thick and pouting, his cheeks red, red.

A real Christmas of a man.

The barman told me to stand by the car for he wouldn't be a moment.

Then he gave me a lift, which I was thankful for because in the lashing air I felt quite drunk and he drove me up the hill and he said: Ah, you're in Gill's Cottage. I told him that Gill was my friend and we talked about his paintings and the other artists who had stayed there over the years and came down to drink in the pub.

The barman came in to see my art then, and only when he was in the cottage with the door behind him shut did I feel like I wanted him out, and like I should never have accepted his lift.

I stood always with him in my view, I lifted and toyed with a brass candlestick that I had visions of stabbing in his eye as the barman looked at the sketches I'd made of a face, which was my face, from studies from an old picture from the time when Alasdair first fell in love with me. I say first, but sadly there was no second time.

I was painting for Alasdair, my love, a present he would never have wanted, and the barman touched the table and said I should light a fire. At that stage I hadn't located the firelighters and the place was freezing but I tried to reassure him that I was fine, and when he asked if I was sure – I think he said that but he slipped into the other language and I was drunk on those two glasses of wine, so sure was something I cannot be – but I said I was fine and I could tell that he was dying to help me like no man ever had, and that also, he was harmless, into the bargain. But I looked at him and suddenly how sensuous he looked around the mouth, how awake he was in the eye when I was not.

Thank you for the lift, barman, I said, you are a good barman and an even better man, I reminded him in case he had begun to have ideas that he was not.

Not a bother of it, he said and he left his number should I need anything.

And when he left I stood frozen, and waited until he was halfway down the hill before I bolted that door with a flimsier lock you could never find. I pushed the sofa against that door after those few moments of not wanting to be afeared and not wanting to be obvious about it.

I pictured the door opening regardless and someone else coming in, someone very different to the barman, and wearing clothes that I could not conjure up, but with a menacing face that I would never forget.

And I busied myself though my head was going, and I tried to rewind back to when I had been in the pub and felt warm and secure, and happy even, to be there.

Then I arranged my hot water bottle, careful so as not to burn my fingers, and I went and pegged towels over the windows and I stood in the kitchen looking for a glass for water to have by my bed, but the kitchen had a large window and no curtain for against it, and no pole, rail nor wire for to peg one to, and I imagined I saw that face looking in at me through the window, and as I walked up the stairs to bed, holding my glass and careful not to miss a step, I thought I saw that face in the corner of my room, and I quickly turned some lights on and turned some lights off until I could see into every corner, then I allowed myself to fall asleep.

The next day was the second lonely day, and I don't know quite what happened, I woke up with a smile on my face. I went downstairs and put some music on. I took down the towels and opened the curtains. I refused to be afeared.

I was not going to be like that anymore, I said aloud, because I talked to myself.

Then I thought about the filling of silence, how it was the cure for my loneliness and I set up my paints, moving my easel to a different part of the room to cease the boredom, but first I showered, not watching for a face in the corner of the bathroom for the first time since Mina left. And not afeared to close my eyes to keep the shampoo out.

And then I dressed, ate, chatted to myself and was happy. I reminded myself of those scenes in American teen movies.

You know, the ones where a boy who has been trying his luck with a girl for a long time, like a week, gets a lay and is so happy that the next morning he wakes up and dances everywhere he goes.

I was slightly like that as I made a playlist from my few downloaded songs and I played it on my phone.

No dancing. But a sure-fire spring in my step when I went for my first walk.

I walked halfway up the hill until I saw a sheep and took a u-turn. Gill had kept saying to me when he first offered me the cottage: Make sure you go the top of the mountain and look down, but as I walked I saw how far it was, and I had climbed mountains before, two of the biggest ones people can climb and I had already climbed them, and that was not what I had gone to the cliffs for. I had gone there to paint. Remembering this, I stood taking photos of the ocean, sheep and rocks, and then I came back down, the intermittent winds and rain had eased and it was quite a cold but beautiful day, and with no intention to lock myself up again just yet, I walked back downhill past Gill's cottage and on down further still until I came to the odd house here and there. I walked on more until the road narrowed and all the while listening to a song that was about someone admitting they had never loved, and I almost stopped on the road at the emotional nudeness of this lyric.

I began to walk in a stop-start manner thinking about those words. Then a car came around the corner and I had to jump up and onto a rock, holding onto the fence, and I made a point of giving the kind-faced older man in the car – a farmer perhaps – a massive smile. I jumped down and was on my way too quickly to see his response, for I didn't need a response. I was all the response I needed that day.

When the road got narrower still I turned and headed back to the cottage a little bit perturbed by the bending and windingness for I would have liked to have gone on all day and walked to somewhere where people were. Then I passed a woman who was standing at her own cottage, she was in her coat and hat and had two bare tongue-red hands with which she was washing the ocean mist from her windows.

I could not hear what she was saying because of my headphones and her slipping into the language, but I assumed she was saying that it was a nice day.

It *is* a nice day, I said in reply and I removed my headphones to hear her but I kept on walking as I did so.

She was smiling like she was really happy to see me and she said something else I didn't quite know but that I replied to with thanks, and added, And you! I don't know why but she smiled at me, seeming to understand, and as I passed by her cottage I noticed the heaviest scent I'd ever smelled of washing detergent, bar squirting it straight up my nose when I was the kind of young girl who did such things.

When I returned to Gill's cottage I was buzzing. I wanted to take the walk all over again, and I did before nightfall, but I was there to work and so I set to it. That was when I found the firelighters, got a patchy reception, a bar or two on my phone, found the YouTube tutorial and texted Alasdair. After his thumbs-up reply, Alasdair called me from work to congratulate me on the fire in five broken up calls that probably held the space of one minute altogether. I told him about the pub and the fire, and that … look, I was there to work, and I was; I was there to concentrate on working and I was; I was getting out of the place exactly what I wanted, I told him and he sounded relieved after I had been so lonely and afeared during the first lonely day. And I said that I had a paint brush in my hand and I let him go, delighted that I was not lonely enough to need him, but forgetting, in my being wrapped up in myself, in the way people are when they are going through trauma, which says something about how unhealing my time at the cottage had been until then, that I was not in the least bit interested in how lonely he might be.

Alasdair had been sending me countless photos on WhatsApp of the dog, which I would only receive when I got the internet through my mobile data which I begrudged using up; and also, I was saving it in case I needed to work out an escape plan.

Gill was coming on the tenth day to bring me to the train station.

And, I suspected, to make sure that I had left the place as I'd found it, which was dirty, dark and warm, but at least now I was working and warmed, at times, by movement, and at other times by my concentration being on hardboard and canvas and not on my skin.

—

39

But Mina had only brought so many briquettes, deciding that we would go out at the midpoint and restock. But at least she left me her food; although I had insisted she take it with her, she had felt so very guilty for leaving she'd said: No, that will do you for food, we are miles away from any town. And she had quickly sorted the cupboards, pushing the perishables to the front and telling me some sort of eating system so that I would not get caught short.

I have always been someone who likes what she likes. I am good to myself, it is how I get over bad things. I never deprive myself because my life has not been easy. Some people work themselves into the ground and for a while I was that kind of woman, but by then I was also someone who knew how to look after myself.

If I had a bad day, I would reward myself with trash TV or a Chinese takeaway and there were neither on the cliff.

I worked all day when there was light enough through the skylight, but when the night came, although I'd had such a great start to that particular day, I felt so very frozen with afearedness that I opened the wine, thinking it had been the thing to help the night before in the pub. And so, I lit a fire and drank and tried to read my book, but I also closed the curtains and pegged up the towels to reinforce my privacy, and every time I had to go into the kitchen I imagined that face looking in at me. I thought about myself not dancing but spring-stepping it about the room earlier that day and I put on my music and I said to myself: You're nearly forty, grow the fuck up! and I took charge. I actively thought about everything that bugged me about the place and I made every change I could. When Mina was there we had not locked the doors.

Someone could have been lurking outside then but I had not given it a second thought or care; why now was it different? I was being silly. I prepared, boiled the kettle, filled the hot water bottle, brought it up to my room and set it in the centre of the bed, then I took another trip and put a cushion in the high, curtainless loft window.

I looked through my boards and took an extra hardboard that I had brought to lean my canvas against, and found that the paint was dry on it so I put it into the kitchen window, it fitted exactly. And I had the wine bottle beside me and made sure I had something on which to set my glass so I would not accidently kick it over and be startled.

And even as I did all these things, I still saw that face in the dark corners of the room. I still was afeared to use the bathroom or go into the kitchen because it had been so very frightening in the night time for a few days already, and it was still somewhere I could hardly bear to be. Even though it was fine in the day, at night that kitchen made me a small thing again, with its rodent repeller plug-in that warned away the mice who I wanted to come in for comfort; the same as the sweet, scared sheep I'd met on the bank for my later walk, and the inquisitive cows who had looked happy to see me on the first one.

I missed a pet, a warm body, and when the fire eventually died and the wine was done, and to my annoyance I was nowhere near tipsy, and the noises that houses make – that I had an understanding of at home – sent absolute terror through me, and all I wanted, or the least of what I wanted, was to climb into the loft and curl up and sleep.

I lay on the warm spot of the bed, and in the dark, worked the hot water bottle down to my icy toes. The bottle was inside a furry case and when I slid my feet beneath it it felt just like my dog, and instead of being comforted I felt quite alarmed, having to turn on my bedside light and look at the water bottle for a face it did not have.

The next morning, I wanted to sleep as I had done the night before, but instead I was unable to get back over when I woke early.

I could not get out of bed, counting the days and realising – in a glass half-empty kind of way – I was only at the halfway point of the stay. I was sorry that when I lost interest in my book I had started to look at my laptop and spent hours looking at photos of Alasdair and our dog, which was why the dog had been on my mind.

I so wanted to have him there, or a little lamb, just milling about the cottage, to come to me and look at me and give me someone to talk to without worrying myself that I was going not-so-slowly mad.

I got out of bed without any spring in my step and went downstairs carrying the luke-warm water bottle, knowing I would have to bury myself in my art. It was not as nice outside as it had been the day before, when it had done me good to walk in the red light of the morning and again in the afternoon just after the redness had subsided, when at four-thirty, just before nightfall, I had briskly walked in the powdery light, and had felt warm both times when I returned and stripped down to a T-shirt. I remembered this, that it blew the cobwebs away, an overdone saying but a true one; I suppose, having lay under the webby eaves for nights I confidently knew a thing or two about them.

Those walks had made me warm and helped my stiff back after relentless, countless hours at the easel, trying to get an eye right on the face I was painting, as I was leaning into that eye and blotting it away to redo it again, over and over. The background had come together well but the detail had not, and when I looked at it that morning with a coffee cup in my hand, trying to stay warm, trying to save the briquettes, I thought of calling the barman and asking him to bring some to me but I could not.

Then I realised that the painting I had been trying to do was all wrong; and I'd been ignoring how I would get it home without the fold-down space in Mina's Land Rover. I looked at the face on the board, it looked deranged.

So, with a wash I blotted it all out, telling myself that the last few days had not been a waste and that I knew now where I had been going wrong. I tried to get back into reading my book as I let the wash dry and then I made a nice easy outline of an eye, and I felt okay, that this time I would do it right. It lingered over me, this uneasy feeling.

I had not followed the new rules I had set myself to survive this place: I had not got out of bed with a bounce; nor listened to music; nor ate with a view to expelling the energy.

I was slow now and sat and ate and felt the loneliness deep within my bones. I thought about thinking the way one can only cut a diamond with another diamond. My mind was the very thing that tore my mind up, or at best left sharp scratches.

That day after lunch, in the mist and mizzle, I saw that bad weather was settling in. The house would howl every night, even after a clear day, which gave me an idea of how bad it could get, so I took the last chance I thought I probably had, and I wrapped my scarf twice round my neck, and zipped up my coat and put on my hat, then I found my playlist on my phone, plugged in my earphones and locking the door, went out for a walk.

The road was wet and the fields sheepless compared with the day before, but I kept my head down with my hood up, concentrating on just getting up the hill, and also on my arc of a skyless view, I carried on, pushing on, although I was heavier that day and it was wetter, but not wet exactly, but grey, and not mystical like the moon could be over the ocean, and not powdery like the grass could be before twilight. It was one-twenty in the afternoon and everything was grey and white as limestone.

I walked on and had an idea for the painting that would help me, a different colour palette, and I took a note in my phone, keeping one glove off. As suddenly as the day before when I had seen a sheep outside the railings on the grassy bank, I saw a figure in grey and whites, the luminous orange piping around his backpack standing out from the grey sky.

That sheep I had turned away from the day before, sensing it was his road and asking myself if sheep could be vicious, would he decide to jump? to jump on me? and hurt me?

Only then, turning away, had I felt much safer, with him behind the bend. But the figure was heading downhill and I reasoned that he was a farmer, but he was too slim and lithe, and a farmer would not wear such a backpack, and certainly not a backpack with such jazzy detail. So I secondly reasoned that the figure was a climber, here to climb the mountain that Gill had been talking about. And that made sense, of course people came to climb it.

There was a cow fence that Gill had instructed me to climb over to get to the top but this was not as far as that point yet, and the man, he looked awfully interested in something in the field and suddenly I had the urge, like with the sheep – as innocent as I knew in my heart that animal was – to turn back.

That same innocence was not in this figure who had come from the field. I could not turn back because I had told myself it was possible to see a person on these roads and say hello, or nod, or even share a car with a strange barman, that it didn't mean they were going to harm you just because you might have been harmed before.

And I walked on and hoped he would turn to his right and that I would be behind him. I took down my hood to look him in the eye and change our outcomes, but he walked past me, suspicious, awkward, and I passed him, saying hello, and seeing his long face, his hat, his dark hair that came out from underneath the hat, the kind that told me he was thin on top, his dead eyes and his mouth full of uneven, spaced out teeth.

I walked on, listening to some song I could no longer hear. I turned off my music for the sound of his steps instead.

Then, unable to look around to make sure he was making his way down toward the cottage, I stopped and did not go any further, for a little bit further on was a corner one could not see around, a corner around which I had not been but knew that it led to nowhere that people could see, and that even from where I was, looking out at the ocean, he, looking back at me, looked even more suspicious.

I made a note on my phone and I took photos of the ocean, and close-ups of the ruins of old cottages, feeling lucky that this is where we had stopped, at a view. I thought it might look as though I had planned it, moving round slightly, not trying to get him in the frame but he frowned as suspiciously at me as if I was.

Had his manner been different I could have relaxed but he crossed the path and climbed the fence, although I did not see him do it. I pretended to look at my phone and I saw a glimpse of him walking through a ruin.

And I walked back toward Gill's cottage which I could see from this height, round twists and turns, and two things occurred to me – no, three – that he could come up from behind me, so I unwrapped my scarf and held it in my hand; that he could be walking under the bank keeping level with me, and I looked around with as relaxed a look as I could manage on my face.

I could not see him at all. I took off my other glove and held my key in my hand like a weapon and I walked; and thirdly, I thought that he might see me walking to the cottage and now I both wanted to be there and not. In fact, I would not leave there for days. I was afeared to go there in case he came looking.

Around the bend I saw a bike that had a rusty, broken chain. Someone had abandoned it and I thought it must have been him, for I had not seen it on the way up, which afterwards gave me cause for concern. And when I looked again I saw him back in the field where I had first seen him, only visible by the orange piping on his backpack. And I finally relaxed.

Gill was coming along the road with his family in the car. I was relieved to see them. They were only passing through, he said, and that he'd been in the cottage to pick up mail and see me for a while, but now they had to go because they had a date with the chocolate factory.

A chocolate factory, I said, having eaten my last piece of chocolate from my stash the night before along with my wine.

And he said: How's it going? Productive? and I said: Oh yes, and inspirational too, and he laughed. I'll see you after four sleeps then, Gill said and he drove off.

And the view of those bodies, all ignoring each other in his car, listening to the radio and feeling the heat seep in through their bones, looked like bliss. Not to mention the chocolate, and I went into the cottage and burst into tears, still clutching the key in my hand.

My terror had subsided, my afearedness of being hurt, of dying. But still the terror was in me and my own thoughts were the worst of all.

The thoughts presenting back to me from before I had seen the man's face; the thoughts presenting to me that should he grab me by the neck and push me up against the bank, that at some point I would let a shudder out of me, like a high-pressure valve released, and that it would be so desirable, and so not a part of his own fantasy, but so much more a part of mine, that it would scare him back. Which had been my first presenting thought when he had jumped down onto my path.

And my next one, worst of all, that once I saw his face, I knew that a shudder would achieve nothing, and I knew this because I could now see that his eyes were too shifty, and that he was not a figure assured enough to do the job cleanly. I knew that my desireful shudder would come absently and remain stuck fast in the frozen part of me that had not thawed with coming here to create, but had only refrosted.

I climbed the stairs into bed and I cried, mostly for the thought of the chocolate, then for the thought that I would not leave the cottage again until Gill returned. That Gill had been the last person I had seen and that I would not see him again for days; that out there somewhere in the hills was a man I hoped I would never again see. I would have to survive till then, cold, hungry, unbrave.

When I stopped crying I had the urge to call Alasdair who I knew would make me see reason and feel better but I had to wait until I was calm, it wasn't fair for him to hear me vulnerable when I was this far away. So I texted him instead.

Of course, when he could he called me back and we chatted it over, he asked me to call Gill before he got too far away, and he asked me to tell Gill that I wanted to go to the chocolate factory too, then Alasdair asked me to go back and talk to the nice woman who was washing her windows, or to even call the barman and ask him for advice on what to do. He might invite you for dinner, said Alasdair.

Poor trusting Alasdair, he did not understand the level of afearness that lived in me, a level that men could never understand unless they'd hid in the trenches, or ever tried to safely detonate a bomb.

And Alasdair had experienced neither of those.

He pretended to put the dog on the phone and in a voice that made me laugh and with words that made me cry, the dog asked, Are you fine, Mummy? Yes, I said, I am. Then tears.

Oh, no, phone Gill now, said Alasdair.

I can't with red eyes like these, I said. I wanted company but I was too vulnerable to have it.

You know if I wasn't working I would come and get you. Why don't you get a bus, or a taxi?

There are none.

It's only four more days, try to enjoy it, you'd been so looking forward to it, too.

Yes, I gulped. I had.

Next I wrote myself a list: Read every book you brought; work like mad; do all your walking inside the cottage; take naps; and, if the worst comes to the worst, call the barman.

I watched out for his light shining at the bottom of the hill for the rest of the time, though it never did. I knew I could not have gone down there, for I was a different woman than I'd been that first lonely night. I looked in the mirror; took my paint brush and I painted my face on the canvas and the word Fragile over it, and then I rubbed my real face inside the outline, one layer over the other, this one made raw with my own painted skin. I painted the background grey and when the face was dry I gave her eyes. Red and puffy for dear, dear Alasdair.

On the day before my last, I almost climbed that mountain but I stopped before I got to the top. I did not need to climb that mountain, because I had climbed enough. I had needed to get past the point at which I had stopped before though, when I turned and ran, but not ran, inside, away to safety; that was the important thing.

I saw the islands and the real farmer who came to feed the sheep, and I saw them as I walked downhill, the sheep on one side with a red paint mark above their eyes, and in the opposing field, more sheep with the same mark but in blue, and all I could think was, Montagues and Capulets.

It is silly how things like that work: popular culture: the things that connect you to the world at large, and to others, and your younger self.

Red and blue dots appeared in my painting, the one I gave to Alasdair that he didn't understand and how could he?

I understood. I understood the world and in turn that felt to me like the world understood me back.

The day before Gill came for me I got an early night, I lay beneath the eaves thinking that maybe I should have wiped away the cobwebs but I couldn't and didn't. At 10 p.m., I thought I heard someone trying to get in the door, and with one tiny window – it was not like at home, where you could look out and see if there was a figure at the door – I could not see out. So I stood up, put the lights on and I called out: Yes, is someone there?

And it could have been someone but I never knew. It could also have been the radiators coming on, but wouldn't I have noticed that all the other nights? Either way, there was no heat, and eventually that awful noise stopped long enough for me to fall asleep.

RECOMPENSE

sender: franart@gmail.com

Jen, you don't know me yet but I am Fran Brady, curator of the A Gallery. I've seen your work: there was a great airport shot of yours in The Notegal Gazette – I don't know how you captured that curious-looking hare so well but I admired the image nonetheless. I would very much like to offer you the opportunity to give a talk here at the gallery. I'm afraid I can't offer you recompense or wall space, as we only show six times a year and are completely booked up for the foreseeable. We already have an exhibition on at the moment (*LIFE!* is an oil painting series by Caspar Roth. Here is the **link** should you want to find out more. Please feel free to share with friends). All that said, I would dearly like for you to come and speak to our regulars, whom we call *Friends of A Gallery*: many of them are also amateur photographers.

(You can become a friend too, for a small fee, there are lots of perks ... Check out this **link** for more information.)

Let me know if any of this interests you.

We could do a slideshow of some of your pieces ...

I'll leave it with you.

Warm regards,
Fran Brady

A Gallery owner and curator

click *here* to read about upcoming group and one person exhibitions

☺

sender: Jenbophoto@gmail.com

Hello Fran,
Lovely to hear from you!

I think the exhibit looks really interesting, I like it a lot and would be honoured to come and speak to the Friends of A Gallery. Just name a time and I will see if I am free.

I am freelancing at The Notegal and part-time at that; just getting back to work after raising my children, so I'm new to the paper (but I'm not an amateur ☺). I've been a professional photographer for twenty years. Where-oh-where does the time go?

My work schedule is hectic. They give the freelancer the jobs that no one else wants; you know how it is! So throw a few dates at me and we'll work it out.

Best wishes,

Jen Beaudette
Freelance photographer

☺

JEN

After a team meeting at the paper, after we have been designated jobs, for the first time my colleague Jonathon Moffat looks me in the eye and speaks to me. Are you looking forward to giving the talk at A Gallery? he asks.

Are *you* a Friend of A Gallery? I ask him in return.

A *friend* of the owner, he says with a smile.

Fran?

Yes, I know her quite well. Been married to her ten years.

You are married to Fran? I ask and he nods. It was through me she got your email address, Jonathon says.

So you are who I have to thank, I say and he smiles and walks off.

I'm surprised; for some reason I thought Fran was a man. More Francis than Frances. Maybe it was the exhibition by Caspar Roth. Now I have to see more about her, so I look up an image and as it downloads I read the text below which reads: *Fran Brady, A Gallery owner, with husband, award-winning photographer Jonathon Moffat.* Then the image appears on my screen and for a second I think the woman is me.

She is standing in front of an easily six-foot-tall canvas, Jonathon by her side. I am simply amazed by Fran's likeness to me, my likeness to her.

The consistencies start with our hair, how we choose to style it, and the colour, they move on to our face shapes, body shapes, the clothes we wear and how, the consistencies go right down to the shoes Fran is wearing; I have those exact same brogues. I go back and read her invitation again wondering if I took her comment about the Friends of A being amateurs 'too' out of context. Now I'm wondering if Jonathon has told her that amateur is what I am. If this is the case, why invite me to give a talk? For a week I have been thinking I must have this artistic eye that I have not known I am in possession of, and now I feel like not giving the talk until my panic text to my husband returns with his insistence that I must. Have faith in yourself, Jenny! he says.

Google Maps shows me that Fran's is a gallery I pass every day when I park in the car park and walk to the office. It is an unassuming little place from the outside, a one-floor premises above the building society.

Inside it is spacious and quite cool. As I arrive through the door with my laptop under my arm, I hear an old man say: I have never heard of this wee girl. I looked her up but she didn't have a website. There was something about her being a family portrait person for a while, if it's the same Jillian.

Then the old woman with him half-turns to me and says: I have never heard of her either, Fran.

I say: No, it's me. I'm *Jen* Beaudette.

Jonathon is here. He is leafing through a programme. When he hears me, he closes it and smiles warmly like he has been waiting for me. His smile makes me come over strange. I think it is a smile that men only give in old movies. Dreamy, transfixed. Like he is going to offer me his arm and we are going to board a train; like we are going to spend the day together by the seaside, away from anyone who knows us.

He has made a big effort with his hair too, I notice this.

What's that you say? the old man asks me.

I'm Jen, I almost shout. I'm here to give the talk.

Jonathon puts down the brochure and smiling similarly at the man he approaches us slowly. Out of a back room comes Fran and it takes my breath away, and then makes me squirm, just how alike we look in the flesh. She shakes my hand, and Jonathon, still smiling says, Hullo, Jennifer. The old man and woman walk off muttering, they sit on two of the thirty seats, the other twenty-eight are empty.

How are you, Jen? Fran says, there is a chive between her front teeth. Thank you for agreeing to do this, she says, I see you have your computer, do you need anything else, a coffee, water?

Water, please, I say and she leaves me with Jonathon.

Sadly we won't have a great turnout tonight, he says.

Oh, that's okay, I say, I'm still happy to be here.

Most of the Friends of A are pensioners, he explains. Fran was saying just earlier that they are all away on some coach trip. I'm sorry, it's just bad timing.

I nod and tremble a little.

Those are my parents, he says about the old man and woman.

They seem like fun, I say.

He smiles the *dreamy* smile again. I don't know where to look. It's creeping me out.

So, how are you finding The Gazette? he asks.

I like it. It's alright.

Settling in okay? The smile becomes more knowing and again I squirm because this is now only the second time we have spoken.

It would help if you and your annoying pals like George and Andy would acknowledge me from time to time, I think.

Settling in fine, I say, remembering suddenly how I had complained in the email to Fran about getting the bad jobs. I wonder if she has told him. She will also know that I have been lying about having to work when I was simply buying time to find some photographs I could pass off as art, and to give her time to find bums for seats.

I'm just getting back into it anyway, I say. My husband has been made redundant; he got a payout that has nearly dried up, that's why I'm back at work. I hadn't planned to be just yet, maybe in another year or so. You get what you can take.

Of course I mean *you take what you can get*.

Yes, Jonathon says. Do you know that Andy is leaving us soon and his job will be free? It's full-time but at least you'd be permanent.

Fran appears by his side with a glass of water. Look, Jen, she says, have a look around while we wait … we'll give it ten minutes more and see if any stragglers come in. Did Jonathon explain about the coach trip double-booking?

Yes, I say. I'm okay if you are. Or I could do it another time …

Or not at all, I think.

It's fine. Not like you're selling anything, she says. Are you?

I shake my head.

Jonathon sits at the back of the room, rows of empty seats away from his parents. I go and look at Roth's paintings, read the brochure about his series; that he is only twenty-two and German. On seeing his photo, I realise I have met him. He has been inside my home.

Caspar Roth came to my door about a year ago. Normally I would send anyone selling anything away but I found that I could not with him, not when he said he was an artist and I heard his sweet but authoritative accent. I brought Roth and his portfolio into the living room where he dished out his canvases on the floor. First he showed me reproductions he had painted of the classics: The Starry Night, Sunflowers, The Mona Lisa, and then he showed me a painting.

Georgia O'Keeffe! I said in response, O'Keeffe meets Jackson Pollock meets Salvador Dalí.

No, Roth said, this is my own original work.

My husband came in then and sat on the sofa. Roth, right at that point, looked me in the eye and said: What do you see here, Ma'am, when you look at this painting of mine?

So I looked harder. A woman? I ventured.

Yes, he said, a woman's genitalia. I am painting a series of them, called *Life!*

And he spread them out over the top of the classics, on my living room floor, and raked his fingers over glossy impasto vaginas. There was something so mesmerising about his voice and his love for his own work, how he looked at it; and his audacity.

Roth had a boyish face that seemed to get more and more handsome every second you looked at it. Then he stopped at one painting he called Flower, which was a smaller version of the biggest painting hanging here on the wall of A Gallery.

My husband said: Do you want the image of the flower, Jenny?

He was working then and has always been so good at looking after me and giving me everything I need and want, which makes me feel slightly sad now when I think how much I have hated working at The Notegal Gazette.

It's a little easier now I don't dislike Jonathon quite so much, but the other photographers are an irritation I could do without: George and Andy.

I am glad to hear that Andy is leaving, he is a grumpy old sod; and George is a huge gossip, really thinks he is something, a Camera Club member who considers himself a trapped artist. And when I think about him I wonder why Fran hasn't asked George, or indeed Jonathon himself, to give the talk. But perhaps her husband is too traditional and I have an industrial edge; a gloom Fran deems inventive.

I actually have this painting. My husband bought it for me, I say to Fran. I don't tell her that it only cost fifty pounds when she is asking for five thousand in her price guide, which is quite the leap, even if it is four times the size. I don't say that after one month I could not bear to look at it and wondered how I'd ever agreed to my husband buying it.

I was quickly embarrassed by Flower. It is now in my loft wrapped up in an old bedsheet.

Oh, Fran says, Roth is really rather good.

And really rather handsome, don't you think? I say.

Hmm. Her face bulges with distaste. I don't know, says Fran and the chive between her teeth catches my eye.

I thought, I say, that he could sell ice to Eskimos. Really charming and handsome like that.

But Fran only shrugs. Then I see a straggler, a woman in a felt hat, come in and take a seat in the second row.

Roth's still finding his own style, I say as if I know what I am talking about, which I clearly don't and this is re-emphasised to me when I go through my own work in front of a gallery owner and her award-winning husband.

My slideshow of airports and old buildings, abandoned warehouses where something bad has happened, places that are about to be bulldozed.

I talk about using black and white to emphasise the despair, and of course: the centre of interest, I talk about possible distractions, enhancing the foreground; all of that.

At the end, Fran opens the floor to questions and the woman in the felt hat seizes a chance to ask one.

Are you Fran's sister? she asks, to which I say, No. Any *photography*-related questions?

And into the bargain, I really hope to learn that Jonathon's father has some respiratory condition, because he has not stopped sighing throughout while Mrs. Moffat Sr. is lifting her husband's arm by the sleeve and consulting his watch every so often.

Then Jonathon says, looking at a spot on the wall: What is the best camera you can buy? and Fran turns to look at him.

It is kind of him to formulate a question even though he well knows the answer, considering he is a good five years older than me and has not had to break career from photography to be a parent; has been able to grab photography by the balls until it has submitted to him the texture of its truth.

The best camera? That is so subjective, I say, there is no doubt that the more money you spend the more sophisticated the camera you can buy, but what is good for me may not be what is good for you.

The woman in the felt hat is nodding enthusiastically at everything I say, and when she catches my eye she looks from me to Fran like a courtside tennis spectator, as if hoping to get me thinking just how much alike we look.

At the end, Fran gives a dynamic round of applause and then presents me with a large bunch of ginger-scented Irish lilies and a bottle of cheap plonk that has been, until now, hidden in the storeroom. She explains that Jonathon has to get back for their boys' bedtime and he disappears without a goodbye. But his father hovers about. Oh, I don't like those paintings on the wall, he says, what are they meant to be of?

A woman, I say and his wife grimaces at me. Her teeth have a lovely light marbling that I really enjoy looking at.

Oh, I don't see it, her husband grumbles. Give me a nice painting of Donegal any day.

A landscape? I ask.

Yes. Johnno takes pictures I like. Yours are odd; don't get offended when I say that.

You can't say that, Jonathon's mother says. That's Jillian's art.

Jen, I insist, and it's really not. Not at all. They are just pictures I've been sent to take after a story has broken. Like I explained during the talk.

A little hare at the airport? You always see that, don't you? It was just good timing. Jonathon's father is happy to have caught me out.

That's a knack too, Jonathon's mother says. Forgive him, please. And what that woman was saying, Christine, the woman in the felt hat …

Yes?

About you and Fran passing as sisters; I said the same thing, didn't I, dear? I thought you were Fran when you first walked in.

You weren't adopted, were you? says Jonathon's father.

I shake my head. Then they leave for their restaurant reservation and the woman in the felt hat comes to chat.

She says, I lovelovelove your work and you are lovely. I want to take you home with me.

Oh, thank you so much, I say.

And not only have you produced wonderful pictures but you are also a lovelylovely person.

She hugs me like she has known me for years.

Oh, you are lovely too; I could take *you* home, I say.

Then she leaves, giving a little wave over her shoulder that she is either certain I will see or doesn't care if I don't. Fran pats me on the shoulder but her hand does not feel easy on me.

Never mind her, she says, Christine comes to all these things, she is here when I open the door in the morning. I have to pretend to be busy to get rid. She's actually a certified lunatic.

I notice that the chive that has adorned Fran's teeth so nicely has worked its way out, making me run my tongue slowly about my own mouth.

☺

FRAN

Fran had asked him to describe her. A lot like you, actually, he'd said and that was all, which was unusual in itself because he normally told her everything about everything. Now that he remained quiet and even defensive to her questions, Fran decided that something was afoot.

In Tesco, she spent twenty minutes buying Jen a gift as recompense for her time. She spent fifteen minutes choosing the right flowers and five minutes deliberating on the bubbly, then Fran went to A Gallery where she prepped the room. Fran was setting out chairs when Jonathon arrived.

Mum and Dad will stop in on their way out for tea, he said and Fran gritted her teeth; she did not want them there. Neither did she want Jonathon, yet it was crucial that he was. Fran wanted to show Jen that they were together and indestructible. What she did not want was to look at her husband at any point and see him looking at Jen.

Who else is coming? he asked.

I had a whole load of people who can't be here now because of a coach trip they're on.

Pity! he said lifting a brochure. Should we take away some of these chairs, then?

No, leave them there, said Fran. She had not told Jonathon that no one had signed up to the Friends of A Gallery scheme yet.

The gallery was nothing like she'd hoped despite all her experience and best efforts. Even the young artist was back in Germany and Fran had no buyers for any of his pieces, not one since the exhibit opened. Roth had come in, smooth-talked her then left her with all this ugly shit.

When Jen arrived, Fran ran into the storeroom to collect herself. She lifted a stale egg and chive sandwich that she had meant to eat earlier and forgotten about with all her faffing about over flowers and champers. She took a bite and watched through the one-way window as Jen stood awkwardly at first and then eased into speaking to Jonathon's parents.

Fran took a drink of cold tea and watched Jonathon walk towards Jen, his back to Fran, who took breath freshener from her bag and sprayed it into her mouth, then she walked out of the storeroom feeling like she was seeing herself speak with her own husband, she rushed toward them in a froth, said hello, and was soon back in the storeroom with Jen's drinks order. From there she tried to watch how they spoke but their expressions were an un-colour; the pair looked at once at ease and yet bored with each other, perhaps they were conspiring together or were just uncomfortable with the position in which Fran had put them in because of the position in which they had put themselves: between a woman and her husband.

In the days after the talking event she felt content. Doing nice things for Jonathon to show him he was already loved, and partly to pierce his lust bubble with remorse.

She stopped thinking so much about Jen, who would now know that she was on Fran's radar. And that should have been enough. It almost was, until Jonathon confided about his dream:

I was in a shop, he said over breakfast and in front of their children. I was waiting in line behind a woman who was standing at the checkout. She was running her hands down over her hips searching for her purse but she couldn't find it.

He was not one for dreams, so Fran listened up.

Then I put my hand in my own pocket and there was a packet of bacon, so I decided I would give the bacon to the woman, to use as legal tender ... of means.

How did it end up in your pocket, Dad? asked the elder boy.

I must have stolen it.

It's bad to steal, said the younger boy, listening now.

Well, yes. Remember it was only a dream and not real life.

Should you be saying this in front of them? Fran asked.

Maybe I didn't steal it, but it was in my pocket – in the dream – and I was thinking that if I was to show it to the woman maybe the cashier would see it.

The cashier? said Fran

The essence of a cashier, with no face.

Like a ghost? asked the younger boy.

Maybe, said Jonathon. If the cashier saw it they would think I'd stolen it, but I couldn't let the woman leave without her shopping and go home empty-handed. She needed my help.

Very chivalrous, Fran murmured.

When the children had gone to fetch their school bags he put his arms around Fran and from behind kissed her on the shoulder. He said, Franny, I am sorry about the cheat dream.

Fran stood in front of the largest painting in the exhibit. Flower, the German had named it. She imagined it on Jen's wall at home, Fran's flowers in a vase beside it, Jen standing, just like she had the night of the talk, looking at Flower, while drinking Fran's bubbly, Fran's man under her skin.

She jumped when Christine suddenly said, I enjoyed that talk the other night. She had a packet of photos with her. Christine fanned the snaps out on the desk, pushing brochures and price lists aside.

I was inspired to go out and take snaps of the airport.

Fran went over to look at them. They are much better than Jen's, she said spitefully.

Oh really, you think so? You are so lovely to say that.

I'm not lovely, I'm honest.

You *are* lovely. You have everything lovely: a gallery and a handsome husband and lovely boys, you deserve every bit of it.

We were in the shops yesterday together, Jonathon and I, said Fran.

Oh, fantastic. What did you get?

Christine's eyes lit up with that childlike enthusiasm that bugged Fran often.

A woman in front of us had forgotten her purse and Jonathon said: I'm going to pay, I can't see her go home empty-handed.

Ooh, isn't he a keeper! said Christine.

What do you think of that? asked Fran.

It's really ... like I said. Then Christine's face dropped and she began to tug on her felt hat. What did you say the woman looked like? she asked.

Erm, said Fran, she looked kind of ... I think she was my height. My age.

Wasn't it funny how much Jen looked like you?

Did she?

Oh, yes. I couldn't believe it. If the woman in the shop looked like that, I don't know ...

If anyone could misinterpret the dream it was silly, stupid, old Christine, thought Fran.

Why would that matter? she asked.

Christine, peering out from under her hat, said: If she was an old dear I would think he was brilliant ... but someone like you, it would be too much. How much did her shopping come to?

Not much, said Fran. That's not the point.

But you need your money, you don't sell any paintings, do you?

It doesn't work like that, Christine; art is different. I don't have to sell something every day. Sometimes one a month covers everything.

But hardly anybody comes in, or I'd see them.

I sell pieces online, too.

Oh, well that is good.

I sold a massive one last night. That one. Fran pointed at Flower.

You should get a sticker on it before someone else comes in.

I was just about to, said Fran in irritation. So what do you think about Jonathon saying he wanted to pay for her shopping? I stopped him but he was thinking about it.

I'm so glad you didn't let him, Fran.

Why?

The woman might think that he was trying to ... *crack* on with her.

He made some joke about paying for her shopping with bacon … because we were buying bacon at the time, said Fran.

Within the compass of a minute, since she'd first mentioned the cheat dream, Fran felt defeated.

It makes me think of the saying, said Christine, bring home the bacon. I've never heard of pay with the bacon …

Fran thought about what it meant, to bring home the bacon; she thought about it when Christine left to take her daily walk around the town in all the shops she liked.

Fran Googled variations of what it could entail

(a) the person who brings home the bacon provides the family with money to live

(b) to succeed

(c) to win

She remembered the conversation she had heard Jonathon having with Jen about her husband's redundancy money running out.

Fran always looked out for Jonathon's photos in The Notegal with a sense of pride, then she had noticed this new name crop up: Jen Beaudette. She let it slide for a while hoping Jonathon would bring her up first.

Oh, she's only a temp. part-timer, he finally said when she asked him. Only there because her husband worked in Aerospace Solutions and was let go. She's trying to be friendly but you can tell Jen doesn't want to be there.

So you talk to her? Fran asked him.

No, I'm out and about myself.

But Jonathon would have gone back into the office for forgotten memory sticks, lenses and the like, at weekends and evenings, like he'd never done before. And often the geographical areas where their photos were taken overlapped.

Fran knew how tight the paper was on mileage.

Did you travel with anyone? she asked.

Just George, he'd say, but often this did not collate with the photographic evidence.

☺

I must say that I thoroughly enjoyed your website, George said and looked at Flower with its tiny red dot that Fran had put on it. Shamelessly the German wanted thousands for it and she had got them, at least for Christine's sake. George lifted a guide and whistled at the price. So, this is the seminal piece, he said. I have some art with me. It's pretty risqué … I'll show you.

If only Fran had as many buyers as she had wishful exhibitors she'd be laughing. She hoped that Christine had not gone off with any such notions.

George was smiling as he set out on her desk colour photos of nudes.

The poses were contrived, and condescendingly snapped from above a sitting, then sprawling, woman. Fran knew what he'd say, that colour adds realism. Silly, stupid, old George, he had found some amateur model he was too intimidated to speak to, obviously foregoing any rapport-building. The model's boredom could not be disguised; the quiver in his hands had left an illuminating blur where skin met air.

This was not the art with which Fran had imagined she would rock her small country: that, since a child, she had pictured as the detachable head of a sleepy teddy bear.

In her early-twenties she'd worked as a gallery assistant on the Southbank, seeing such great exhibits that caught her eye along the way that she picked them up like stones to build her own imaginative waymark.

Fran's dream of her own gallery back home began with an exhibition by photographer Antoinette Robinson. Antoinette took the most beautiful shots, all in black and white. They were mainly lines and contrasts on the greyscale. Sensual and tender at once.

The exhibition's title was: From the First Breath to the Last. Everything about those close-ups worked; that you could only see what you wondered was a closed eye or an open mouth was all the intrigue you needed. The models could almost have been anybody. Indeed when they came to the exhibition launch clothed ordinarily, no one even knew it was them.

Antoinette Robinson had made something so intriguing from the human body and those pieces Fran could not unsee.

They had stayed with her until she opened A Gallery (named for Antoinette, and also to distance her own name from the venture should it not work out, which seemed to be the way it was headed) and Fran got more and more depressed by the day that a local Antoinette Robinson did not walk in off the street to offer up their work; that any would-be buyers would walk around wrinkle-nosed at the walls, muttering and mumbling, If you had a nice Donegal landscape or something like that I would buy it.

Fran doubted it, double-doubted it when she opened up the tab on her computer with Jonathon's website of just what they claimed they were after, and still, nose wrinkles! But to buy art like that? Or some, so they claimed, on a complimentary colour scheme to match the cushions? They were not her target buyers.

As for George, he was only slightly sealed with the stamp of creativity. But good on him, Fran thought, he'd served his purpose of getting a woman's kit off without buying her dinner, and bringing those pictures to his friend's wife, pretty excited to be there in those charged surrounds; in the world seen through Roth's eyes. In … *LIFE!*

George was not Roth either, who at least thought he had something to offer, and had an answer for everything she tried to throw at him.

And that smile! The homewrecker had a point with her Eskimo and ice remark.

What are you trying to get over here, George? Fran asked.

I was trying to get the light. See here, he said, against her hip. I was trying to … here, you can see where the light penetrates and …

What is the essence of it, your series?

Light and the human body.

Fucking, really, isn't it? Fran said. It's impossible to talk about art without talking about fucking.

That's why you have pussies all over the wall?

That's it, that's exactly why, she said.

She could tell he had decided not to hear her irony.

So if I take some more photos, you'll give me your critique? he asked.

I will, but you give me your opinion first.

What on?

What has gotten into Jonathon lately? asked Fran.

How do you mean?

Don't tell him I'm saying this, but he is insatiable. He wants sex all the time.

George shielded his eyes as if he had walked outdoors into a shockingly sunny day.

Why do you think that is? Cos I know how you boys talk …

Maybe he just thinks you're gorgeous.

Don't repeat this to him. And definitely don't say anything to Andy … or the new girl.

Who? *Jen?*

Yes.

I believe you had her here to speak, said George.

Fran could see he was jealous. I did, she said smugly. She's lovely, isn't she?

I thought she was you … the first time I saw her. But I don't see her photos as anything other than bland.

He let the last word drop out of his mouth like old chewing gum.

I heard that you don't talk to her.

She's married.

So? Aren't you talking to me, now? I'm married.

It's different.

She needs someone to take her under their wing at the paper, said Fran. Gosh, I don't know what she'd think of Jonathon if she knew what he's been like lately. *Insatiable*.

I don't know what you're concerned about anyway, sounds like you're both at it like rabbits.

Did he see these photos of yours?

Yes, said George.

And he liked them?

Jonathon said, *yeah, go ask Fran.*

George, said Fran, there was a woman in here earlier, the woman who bought that painting.

She pointed at Flower.

Rich woman, then, said George.

She was telling me the weirdest thing. That this morning her husband admitted he'd had a cheat dream.

George laughed.

You've heard of that before? What is it?

It does what it says on the tin.

But is it a new phrase? I've never heard it.

It's where you dream about having sex with someone who isn't your partner. Why, Fran, have you never had one?

Like I'd tell you! I know what a gossip you are. You'd only end up telling everyone at the paper. Including lovely Jen ... But this woman, who bought the painting, said that her husband told her he had one.

What a stupid man.

I thought he'd be sleeping with someone else, in his dream, said Fran, but all he did was stand behind a woman in a shop and when he saw that she had no money, he thought about paying. He put his hand in his pocket and there was no money, but there was bacon, and he wanted to give this to her but he couldn't without getting found out.

Found out for what?

Well, it must have been stolen because it was in his pocket.

Oh, I see, said George. Because it was in his pocket. Right ...

So what do you make of that, as a man?

He's only told her half of the dream.

That's what I thought, too.

She must have liked it anyway, the wife.

Why do you say that, George?

She came straight here and bought this. George nodded at Flower.

Oh, I don't think the two are linked, said Fran. Maybe he felt bad and gave her the money, but the woman did say that she was buying it for herself.

I find that very hard to believe.

Oh? said Fran.

A woman, buying that kind of thing for herself?

Why's that so hard to believe?

Even though it's so graphic?

It's abstract, she argued.

It's not *that* abstract. It says everything about fucking that my photos don't.

And what about the bacon? she asked. I was thinking it could be a symbol.

It's a luxury item, said George. Not something you eat every day … It's a treat.

Her husband wasn't eating it, but yeah, that's another element … I was thinking, *bring home the bacon*. He was taking it from his pocket and giving it to her.

I'd be more concerned – if I was the wife – about the pocket than the bacon, said George and Fran's jaw dropped slightly.

Was he wearing a jacket in the dream? he asked. It could be his inside pocket which means he's giving the woman …

His heart.

There you go! Or, it could be his trouser pocket, in which case the husband's fucking her, really, isn't he? The woman in the line.

I bloody knew it! said Fran. That homewrecker!

And then, said George, he goes and gives his wife five grand recompense, and she goes out, buys herself a new painting. But isn't that good news, Franny? I mean, you get the sale, and the German gets to eat for a while. Everybody's happy!

REGARDING JACK HENRY

AFTER SHOOTING OFF a pissy email to Pin at the WAB, I succumbed to a sleep I thought I might never wake up from, counted my options in the currency of dreams. Dreams that chased me into a warren of further and even more wearisome dreams, inside which I could not decide if I had a case against Mr. Henry at all.

The thing is, that I have slept almost solidly since September, and that is also to be taken into account when I get talking with Pin, who has kindly and promptly replied to my email, making me an afternoon appointment that I just about manage to wake up in time for.

I must remember to thank her for that. When I am in my car, stopped at the traffic lights, I make a note on my phone in case I forget.

The cars around me have back seats filled with Christmas boxes. I give the driver next to me a dead-eyed look I lately can't help but give, yet despite this she offers me a sympathetic smile, and on the lights changing nods her head in martial fashion as she cuts in front.

Have you got a claim? it says on her bumper sticker, and I realise she has been sent to see that I arrive at the WAB without conking out at the wheel or taking a detour to my mother's house or weaving off absent-mindedly to campus.

Recently the WAB leaves its logo off publicity material such as bumper stickers – but now and again you still see them winking at you. The source in this one has not gone unrecognised. Someone has scratched the words *look back bitch* just below, into the enamel.

When we get to the Women's Action Bureau, which is just off-centre in town, the woman from the car walks by my side. Holding up, alright? she asks in a feathery voice.

Not great, I admit.

You've come to the right place, she tells me, Pin is amazing.

So she is not Pin. And Pin is still, for the next three minutes at least, an intangible being that one cannot envisage but only think of as a non-human entity.

I walk with the woman through this building, a brutal building that was once the barracks and later a history museum, and I think about Clover Morris and all the work she did here. Clover was still *only* a hot, young, parliamentary personality when she had already spent years blotting out the buzz of her much older male counterparts, who loved nothing more than a good Look Back: men who not only made decisions on women's lib without a woman being present in the room, but also expected Clover to nod her head and never disagree when they told her of their (in)action plan.

During this time she had the foresight, and patience, to nod where nods were apt and agree, without really agreeing with anything, and just when the male politicians thought they had her on side, they decided – in a desperate bid to curry favour with first-time voters – to use Clover's favourable attributes of being youthful and 'equipped', and put her centre stage. But bolstered by an underground force that we today know as the WAB, Clover ended up being elected as First Minister, and from her heights she sanctioned funding for the WAB and renamed the museum, the Men's Museum of Looking Back.

Clover wasn't being sexist with the name as the building only contained artefacts pertaining to males. A visitor from Mars would have thought that women were as alien to this place as they themselves were.

Barely anybody visited the museum during that period; most people made a good attempt to only Look Forward, so Clover Morris closed the place down, declaring there would be no more toxic looking back, and she made the premises the HQ for the WAB. Taking a step back, she left Pin Greer to steer the bureau onward. Which brings us up to today, and makes me think about her most recent interview, in which Clover states that at one stage life in parliament got so boring that she considered taking her own life.

I am happy to say that this no longer occurs to any women here, but the rates for men – bad as they already were – have now hit endemic proportions, and no one wants to see that, I believe; not if the human race should hope to go on. And I believe we want it to.

My good friend Aprille-Mae reminded me recently that there are still plenty of men left in developing countries and that they are not burdened by the issues the men from here are – though of course they have their own, was my conclusion. Aprille-Mae says, she read somewhere, that should we feel the need to procreate – as is often the urge in women who do not fear raising boys to be Looking Forward men – then there could always be Love Holidays to developing countries. She had spoken to someone who had spoken to someone who had read in *The Grapevine* that the WAB is already hotfooting the idea with an action plan, male screening service and government funding.

It is a Love Holiday I am thinking about when I am introduced to Pin by Pin herself: a patrician woman in her sixties with a means-well handshake and a red tailored trouser suit that makes a crackling sound as she walks, leading me into her room just as the hour and minute hands respectively hit north.

I respect your time, Pin says, that you will have somewhere important to go after here and you'll have important work to do.

Thank you, I say, wanting to get the note on my phone out of the way before I forget it. It's refreshing to have someone respect my time like this, I add, though I wouldn't call going home to finish my kitchen plan for CAD class important. But it does have to be handed in before the break, so …

I will not ask you what brings you here, because you wrote all that down in your email and I read it, says Pin.

Thank you for that, I say.

Have you had breakfast or lunch? I bet you haven't.

You bet right.

Pin goes over to a tray, she whips off the sheet that covers it and underneath is a variety of food: granola, cereal bars, fresh fruit, steaming warm sausages and a mirror-shiny chocolate cake. She beckons me over. My hand finds its safe spot hovering over the fruit.

If it was me and I was new to this, says Pin, and I'd been having the time you've been having, I would want cake. But, I would be thinking about keeping my strength up so I would want granola.

Yes, maybe granola, I say.

I would probably lift an apple, says Pin, which is nothing really, is it?

I suppose.

I would do that for appearances, says Pin, so as not to look greedy; imagine people knowing that a woman eats food! But do eat, that's rule number one, and it may not seem like it is related to your claim inquiry but believe me everything is.

Thank you, I say all befuddled.

Pin lifts a plate and I notice she is smiling to herself. I see that you are more ingrained than I thought, she says. You sounded tougher in your email.

She lifts a little of everything onto the plate and does the same to another plate, sets them both on the desk. One for me and one for her. Thank you, I say and I sit behind the plate of food and look at Pin as she eats a slice of cake.

A little of what you fancy does you good, have you ever heard that saying?

Of course, I say and I peel a banana even though I can see the pleasure on her face from the cake and how she is brushing off her hands and the crumbs are going everywhere, making water pool on my tongue. There is a knock on the door and a young sandy-haired man brings us coffees on a tray. You're a coffee drinker, he says.

Oh yes, I reply.

That's the student way, he says asking if I would like milk or sugar.

Ralph, just leave them both, says Pin, we have an indecisive one here.

Thank you, I tell him and Ralph says I am welcome, and Pin thanks him too and he tells her she is welcome too, then he goes out with the tray under his arm.

Pin knocks her black coffee back then puts her cup down. Try to relax, Susan, she says. You are not the one on trial here, please remember that.

Okay, thank you.

You don't need to thank me for stating the obvious.

Okay.

So now, pour your coffee and take a sip and we'll get started.

Th … I stop myself.

Self-consciously I pour milk into the cup and I'd like sugar but have deprived myself of sweet drinks and empty calories for the last two years and shouldn't start now just because it's here. But what I'd really like is cake so I tell myself a sugar cube will do instead of cake, and plus I ate a slice of buttered ginger cake last night.

The reality is that I have no problem eating cake, it is the doing it in front of people that I find so crippling. But I did not come here to think or talk about this. I came here to talk about Mr. Henry.

So, Ralph, I say, is he the token man at the WAB?

The token man? Pin laughs. Whatever gave you that idea?

I thought that only women would work here.

Let me ask you something, Susan. When you were little and had to go to the hospital and most of the female employees were nurses and most of the doctors male, did you like that?

Not exactly.

And when you were at primary school and the principal was a man and the teachers all women, in hindsight are you comfortable with that?

Not in hindsight, no.

So there was this imbalance you have grown up with, says Pin.

Hasn't everyone grown up with it? I ask.

Yes, that is a good point you're making, but you see, studies show that while people like change they don't want to change, so how do we solve this imbalance conundrum?

By changing ourselves?

Superb, says Pin. Have another sip of your coffee and actually, I'll turn the heat down a bit because I can see that you are still quite sleepy.

Oh no, I say, I hope I don't look it, I'd hate to be rude. And Pin … I am finding this very interesting.

Really?

Yes.

You don't expect a lot, Susan, do you?

Erm … I say, then I think for a while before I add, I think it's because of boyfriends who have let me down, and the family members who I can't stand to be around; then there are friends who have stabbed me in the back. I suppose I don't expect anything.

Good, says Pin. We need to be honest about ourselves before we can look sideways at others. And then, you can raise your expectations of people.

She uses a ruler to reach over and lower the temperature gauge on the radiator. I push back my shoulders and try not to slouch, try not to yawn. Now I'm yawning.

Don't worry, Susan, says Pin, the disappointmentation ratio is less for those with higher expectations. You understand that humans are humans and that they will still fuck up, but you will be around better people who are less likely to.

Of course, she adds, you get the bleeding hearts who love the thought of our organisation, they love to fight, they're the type who rebel, all because they never saw their father with a vacuum cleaner in his hand and they never heard a swear word cross their mother's lips.

That's why? I ask.

The research is all there. She nods at a booklet. You can have a copy of *The Grapevine* to go.

That would be nice.

It's not, actually, says Pin, it's pretty awful reading, I'm not going to lie, but I hope you appreciate my honesty; my expectation setting. She winks.

I really do.

I know that, because I read your email and that was what I read, about how much you hate to be disappointed and that is a very legitimate dislike.

Yes? I was worried you would think I was being precious. A snowflake …

And aren't snowflakes precious anyway?

I love them!

We have one life, Susan, and I know it's a saying and quite possibly technically it isn't even the truth, but it also helps to put things into perspective sharpish, don't you think?

Utterly.

If you think about it, it does, says Pin.

I agree, I say.

Yes, you do agree, but please, won't you let me know when you don't. I'm just concerned that – and I would never blame the victim! – but that sometimes being too agreeable is an invitation to the kind of behaviour you have been experiencing.

So you think it is *my* fault?

Not at all, says Pin, you just need to be more self-aware, that's all. You're young, you've got time. We're all still figuring this thing out since they finished collating the data.

I nod at Pin who is eating the granola.

It's good to eat when you're hungry, you know. She nods at the banana I half-peeled then forgot about. We've stopped listening to our bodies, says Pin, and we are overworked, underfed, drinking too much, either not sleeping, or in your case, sleeping our lives away because of the problems stemming from the Look Back era.

I rarely drink these days, I say.

But you use marijuana, or coke?

No! I hate drugs. Personal reasons.

What do you think, Susan? Do we need to stop reading books on how to listen to our bodies and start *reading* our bodies?

Yes, I reply enthusiastically, that makes sense.

You say that as if it's the first time you think I have made sense.

No, Pin, not at all.

Honestly …

I don't know, I say. I've been brought up to think a certain way. I know that what you're saying makes sense but if I can't see it for myself then how can I get past the thing I'm here for.

Give it a name, Susan. Come on, hit me with it.

The …

Say it; you are amongst friends.

The … I can't say it.

The boredom, Pin says, it's an easy word.

The boredom, I say then drink my coffee. Shocked by its sweetness I almost spit it out.

And you are bored elsewhere?

No, that's the thing, I say. I have always managed it well. I've grown up in a house where I was set in front of the TV while my mother did chores that could have been avoided, in hindsight. My father *never* acknowledged me.

Timeout: let's not go too far back, says Pin. That is Look Back territory and this environment is not equipped.

It's good that you are honest about that because some people, I feel …

Say it, Susan!

Some … men?

Pin nods proudly.

Some men would listen to me and take my money and let me ramble.

That has happened before. They've been Look Backists, claiming they weren't.

Yes, I went to therapy, thinking *I* was the problem.

Susan, when I said that had happened before I wasn't asking you, I already have the information from your email.

Thank you for that.

Thank you for what, for doing my job?

Yes.

Thank me in a few weeks, once you are sleeping through the night and only through the night.

Okay.

Alrighty, let's rewind again. Cautiously. Look back only to look forward … So, are you bored elsewhere?

No. I've thought about this and examined that, because of my earlier life, which I'll not get into here.

Pin nods proudly.

I had to cope with a massive amount of boredom and as a result, I actually think I developed a great imagination.

Good work! she says. That's why I don't go there. I am a trained psychotherapist in my full-time job, and we *could* go there but that would be a conflict of interest and unethical, so it is not that I don't want to help you go there, but truthfully, this is a non-profit, and we only make Look Forward change. I don't cross over with the people who I give WAB advice to, nor with the people I give therapy to, okay.

You are really incredible to have the other job too, I say.

Well, I am quite strict there, Susan. You have to be. I get paid well for my main job; that buys me time to do this.

So you don't like your other job?

One life, Susan. Do you think I would waste it on something that didn't give me something back?

I love that, and I just want to say that I admire women like you and of course like Clover Morris.

Clover suffered the boredom so you would not have to, always remember that. They used to say that women were meant to suffer; meant to be selfless. You know, beauty is pain, *blah!* Susan, I took jobs I hated, ones that made me care for people: wash them, cook for them. I'm contractually obligated to say, if you *are* someone who delights in bathing and feeding people – be you a woman *or* a man – go and follow that desire. But this is where self-awareness comes in.

Yes.

Know yourself, set boundaries, know what you want, go and get it. Do not be afraid to fuck up, Susan.

Thank … yes. It all makes sense.

It does when you give yourself time to absorb it.

Maybe that's what I need, I say.

Some people take a month, says Pin, and they go away or even stay at home and they think about that list I just reeled off. It's all in the literature that I hope you will take home with you.

Maybe I will go away for a while.

Why not? Go away and sleep less, stay awake, think about your one and only life.

The door knocks and in comes a different young man, he has a brown paper parcel that he sets on the table.

Apologies, he says, you wanted this as soon as it arrived.

Thank you, Pin says and the young man smiles and says hello to me and I return his hello and I smile a smile I have to hide behind my coffee cup.

Pin says: Please don't think me rude but I have been waiting for this forever. She opens it and adds: Actually, it might interest you, Susan.

I sit forward and watch as she takes from the package a blade that at first I think is a knife, then out she pulls a white leather ice skate, and then another. I hear the door close behind me and the young man is gone. Wow, they are heavy, wanna feel how heavy? asks Pin, and I, always wanting to be no trouble, to keep out of the way and stay quiet, feel inclined to say no thank you, but now I know this is wrong and also rude.

Recently I have learned that sometimes you should just say yes, and take the mince pie you are offered at Christmas; someone has bought the ingredients and been excited for you to call and have one. I have learned that in many areas I should just do what I want, but I can't even think now.

I don't know myself.

I only know that I once loved to skate and that this white boot and its identical sister are pretty to the point of mythical.

I have been disallowing myself the liking of pretty things, things that are not purposeful, things I have judged as being extra-curricular.

I have been all work and no play and I have also been trying to be one of the boys, which hasn't been working on the architecture course.

I am the only woman left on it and barely holding on.

When Mr. Henry, who I am here to put in my claim about, calls out our Maths scores he calls everyone by their surname and adds a Mr. to the front, including to my name, and I am *sick* of him not realising that I am a young woman. One who pains herself to be pretty for our lectures, one who gossips with Aprille-Mae about certain young men who sit next to me, men who I find neither attractive nor interesting; but I have been conditioned to act this way.

Who the fuck am I? I am leaning over the desk and Pin is handing me the ice skate.

Seriously though, Susan, she says, isn't it heavy?

It is, I say remembering the drag of my feet across the rubbery floor of the rink before I would get to the ice, how the first time I ever skated was at Aprille-Mae's birthday party; it was girls-only and we were eight. I hung on to the edges, determined to crack this nut of staying vertical, not speaking to anyone, not even if they spoke to me.

When my mother came to collect me, Aprille-Mae's mother told her that I had just skated and skated.

I've honestly never in all my days seen such determination, she said. Susie didn't play once, just skated the whole time. She got pretty good, too!

On my next birthday, I asked for ice skates and I got a preloved pair for £20 that had been barely worn by a neighbour's daughter, and I postloved them, even wearing them at home on the kitchen tiles, imagining I was on ice.

When I got a little older I went to lessons conducted through school; then I would go on Friday nights with friends until they shut the local rink down.

I had never loved anything so much as I loved the cold air and the feeling of gliding.

I remember the bigger kids whizzing past, and me learning to skate faster so I could attempt to take part in Speed Skate: a time when the novices had to get off and stand stoppered on the rubber floor.

I desired so badly to be good enough to speed skate, and backwards. But we were only allowed to Look Forward.

Wow. I had forgotten how skating was the most favourite of all my delicate pursuits.

Do I want to be a professional ice skater? I ask myself now, knowing in the next instant that that ship has both sailed and sank, and that I don't have the strength or know-how to hold this woman's body upright. I am not a little whizz-about creature anymore.

These are for my daughter, says Pin. It's her birthday tomorrow. Do you think she'll like them?

Yes, I say and I set the ice skate down and gulp. Very nice.

Pin sets them under her desk. Sorry about that, I'm a little bit excited, she loves to skate and I love to watch her loving to skate.

But there's no rink nearby anymore, I say.

Oh, there is if you know where to look. It's all in the literature, she says. Now let's get to business!

That would be good, I say now that I need to refocus on something.

This lecturer of yours …

Mr. Henry.

Mr. Henry?

Yes, a man.

Okay, timeout: I have to stop you there, Susan. I detected some hostility in your voice when you said the word 'man'.

Oh, I … did you?

I did, Susan, and it's not helpful.

Sorry.

Don't … don't apologise. All these apologies and thanks and yeses and noes they stop the flow. It's a bad but breakable habit.

So I say nothing? I say, quite annoyed now.

No, but the opposite! Say something. Pin smiles sadly. Have you ever had a conversation with Mr. Henry?

No.

I can't do this.

What? I ask.

This Mr. Henry b-s. What is his first name?

Jack.

Okay, you see that's what threw me. Not his gender, but his title. From what I see, Mr. is not on his birth certificate.

Oh.

Susan, what age are you?

Twen-ty, I say as if I am asking her.

You are twenty: an adult, and he wants you to call him Mr. Henry, does he?

Yes.

Unbelievable. Does he call you Ms. Winslow?

No.

Well, see, there is the imbalance, says Pin.

But he is the tutor.

So? You are here to see me in a professional capacity and I am not asking you to call me Dr. Greer. I'm not even asking you to call me Mrs. Greer, nor Ms. Greer, nor have I said: actually, it's Mabel-Anne. I'm giving you the common decency of telling you: I am Pin, because when I was a kid I was pin-skinny. Pin is who I have always been. If you said Mabel-Anne I wouldn't even respond because it's not me, you see?

Yes.

So, Susan, what I'm asking next is have you ever had a conversation with Jack Henry?

No, but just to get back to what you were saying about titles, he calls me *Mr.* Winslow, does that count?

Mr. Winslow?

He assumes I am a male because the rest are – it's a weird dance. A weird shitty dance.

And Jack's a maths tutor?

Yes.

So he will argue probability.

Yes, he might.

And you have had no conversation with him?

No, like I said, no.

It's just, maybe … do you think … because you are so agreeable, someone like Jack Henry could indeed, theoretically, say that you are boring to him?

What? No. He doesn't ever remember when he reads the scores out, humiliatingly – that can't be humane, can it? – that he has one Ms. in his class. He can't remember me. Every time.

Jack Henry would not forget you, Susan, for the reason alone that you are the rose in the thornbush, awful saying! You know of it?

Rose between two thorns. I've heard of that.

It's a sexist one alright but that's the way he'll be thinking.

It makes a particle of sense, though I haven't seen him check me out or anything, I say.

What age is he, don't say … 60 plus?

Yes.

Pin looks at me strangely. As long as he is not overt in his checking out of you then that is something you can manage, she says.

Okay, I say.

Can you?

Yes, no problem.

So it is primarily the case of Jack Henry being boring.

That is primarily the case, yes, but also, you made a point with the title thing, the rest of our lecturers are first-namers. And they are wittier; less shouty. But Jack Henry I can't cope with anymore.

Why not, Susan? Give me details. Pin lifts her pen.

He has a voice that he purposefully keeps monotonous, he's a bit of a theatrical guy.

And class is his stage?

Right, I say. So then comes a big booming voice if you fall asleep in his class. He does it on purpose; makes you sleep so he can wake you up.

And he has done this to you, personally.

Well, no.

And … he does it to the others?

Yes.

And you have fallen asleep in his class?

I have. Every class.

And he has seen you do this?

Yes, I think so.

A man like Jack Henry, says Pin, he would see a sleeping twenty-year-old woman, believe me. He'd be attuned to that.

So what do you think? I say.

I think that he doesn't shout at you because you *are* a woman. He maybe sees someone else, another student looking down at his desk, or yawning and he shouts at him, because Jack Henry can't bring himself to single you out.

Really?

Oh I'm certain. The rest of the female students have left the course you say?

Yes.

Pin shrugs. Why?

I think of the course being filled fifty-fifty at the beginning. That is, after all, the admissions criteria. The prospectus always uses the same image of a young woman on a field for every formerly male-oriented course.

Even the old architecture journals in the library were printed with the foresight of using women in all their advertising too, in a *Clover Morris heads up the party so vote for us, newbies!* way.

There would always be a young, pretty woman front and centre. Always. But when you read the names below you would find out that she was never an employee.

I tracked down one of the university's old newsletters with its architectural supplement that featured a study visit from a university in Russia. In the accompanying photo were five men in navy-blue bomber jackets and jeans, all standing in a field looking at a point that could have been a wonderful Russian design or a place where one would be, a place one would have to leave up to their imagination. To the left of the image, a woman in black looked straight at the camera.

Her right foot was pointed at the ground and her hands poised like she might spin off the page, a smile on her pretty, tilted face.

If you do not know anything about Russia back in the Look Back era, you would not know, like I do, that she is not and was not an architect but a well-known, at the time, ballerina.

This kind of thing was the Look Backists' admission of guilt; that they knew they could not leave women out, at least superficially.

I tell Pin that the female students who left our course all said it was not the right course for them. They wanted something with people, teaching …

They fell back into their stereotypical expectations, says Pin. Jack Henry scared them back to the nurturing arms of primary school classrooms where bosoms rule?

Yes.

And you want to be there, in Jack Henry's class because you have always wanted to be an architect?

I wanted to be an artist but that's not a real job, I say.

Pin frowns. It's not?

Architecture is art, only with purpose, and great money at the end.

Pin lifts her blank page and a pen. Susan, take this pen and this page, she says. I'm going to leave you here for five minutes and you are going to write about this: Why am I doing my course? Don't think, just write. Tell me the answer.

Tell *you*? I say.

Eventually, says Pin, first let your heart tell you.

Pin leaves and I sit and write the heading and I don't know what to write. It's hard. It's impossible. But what can I do? Do I refuse to listen to my heart? I can't.

So I continue:

Reasons

1) because God knows what would happen to my mother if I left her with my father and I went away and studied art

2) my mother would be proud and surprised by my choice (she thinks art is relaxation and a hobby)

(she'd be prouder if I was a midwife, or teacher – something meaningful/caring)

(But an architect? Even better!)

3) my father would see me as a powerful person and not a little girl.

(he would notice me? you think?)

4) I would be thought of as intelligent

(one day, I might be someone's boss)

5) I would stay close to my boyfriend

5) I am afraid of the unknown but less afraid of staying here, even though I know I would be better going away

6) I don't want to start hating art because it becomes work, studying art might do this???

Pin comes back and examines my list, she scores out all the mother and father things.

That's a song that can be sung on another day, she says. Remind me before you leave and I'll recommend a therapist colleague for you.

Lovely, I say, embarrassed, exposed. Awake.

My synopsis is that you have no interest in architecture and you stayed for a man. Why have you scored that one out about the boyfriend?

Because, he broke it off with me three days after freshers' week, I say.

Let me guess, does he go to this university you are at?

Yes.

How do you feel when you see him?

Like there is battery acid in my stomach.

Susan, I've been crossing boundaries and I'm going to get back on track because this is more therapeutic than WAB usually offers.

Thank you.

Maybe take that week out, the holidays are coming, think about what you want. Consult your list and the literature.

Is that us done? I ask.

Absolutely not.

I don't want to take up too much of your time, I feel like I know now what I have to do.

You think it's that easy, says Pin.

Hopefully it is.

You are young.

Don't say that, I hate it.

Pin smiles. Why do you hate it?

Because it's like I have to be in my thirties before anyone will see me as a person.

Take the next decade to not take everything so seriously. What's your rush? Or be like Clover Morris, listen, nod and surprise them all.

I sigh. Jack Henry? Do we give up on him then, now I know I'm not going back, and I'm not. I'm no architect.

This man is still a menace whether he menaces you, the other students or the young women getting ready to take that course, says Pin. We can still put in a complaint about him.

Can we?

Oh sure, he has all the traits of the classic case: Jack Henry is entitled, yes?

Yes.

Entitled to be above people, to ignore you, to make fun of your gender?

I suppose.

Is he rude, obnoxious, and does he publicly humiliate people?

Males.

That's all part and parcel … he has a secretary?

Yes.

A woman?

Yes.

He'll be abusing her or screwing her or both.

Oh, I'm not sure, I say and my stomach starts to hurt.

Trust me: he will.

So what do we do?

Let me check. Pin goes to her computer and keys in some details. So what did you think of the man who brought in the skates?

He was nice.

He's my son.

So you have two children?

Three children. I've been married for thirty years. I know that men from Jack Henry's generation have a hard time because my first husband was a *Jack Henry* which gives me great insight, but I also know that they can change their ways.

Did he? Your husband?

Yes, in fact. And we are great friends now, Pin says.

And what about your second husband?

He is brilliant, so I know that men can be good, that's the thing. If I have found a good one then there are good ones to be found. You have to look back, unfortunately – small l, small b – and determine what they got away with.

Pin looks at her computer.

As I thought … Jack's mother is still living. Margaret Henry: sadly no biographical details on her exist but I can more than safely deduce that she was a homemaker devoted to her son.

Do you have that kind of information?

He's on the database, he has been investigated before but nothing came of it. The MAB blocked it. But the law has changed.

What was he investigated for?

I can't divulge. Nothing massive, but substantial enough to have caught our eye.

Is he married?

Twice: once when he was young, and he remains remarried.

Oh.

Susan. You can say it …

Say what?

That it's like me, says Pin.

No, I wasn't going to say anything. I wasn't thinking about anything.

You want to be taken seriously then speak.

Okay, I say. I grew up in a house where I only wished my parents would split, find new people and be let everybody be happy. Some girls dream about wedding dresses, or horses, but a divorce was my dream.

As I say it I wonder at the truth of it. *Did* I dream about divorce? Maybe I dreamt about ice skates.

That's very mature, Pin says.

I hope so.

People fuck up, remember. She points at me.

Yes, I remember.

And you will, too.

I know, I say. I have.

So, here is the WAB action plan most suitable to your claim: we are going to warrant a Harm Code to Margaret Henry, because she'll have been telling Jack all his life that he is her prince, he is wonderful, and actually here is a newspaper clipping where Jack Henry won a beautiful baby competition and he is wearing a bonnet. Exhibit A, we'll call it.

Oh, I have to see this.

Unfortunately I can't show you it, but maybe a copy could find its way to you. Pin winks. She looks back at the computer. His father is dead. I expected that. A Royal Navy Captain; he would have been stern, which was equally as bad for young Jack Henry as his mother's coddling.

I'm starting to feel sorry for him.

Jack has quite the history of womanising.

Really?

And you thought he hadn't noticed you!

I hoped he hadn't …

Maybe you hoped he had so he would go easy on you. In fact, the young men on the course probably have it harder than you because he sees them as virile, and they will know how to talk to women like he does not, and they're at the start of their lives, without the eff ups.

I wouldn't say they know how to talk to *me* …

But you went to an all-girls school, correct?

How do you know this?

It was evident when my son came into the room.

How? I blush.

You have learned that a man will only talk to you if he is trying to get into your pants.

I …

I know, Susan, it gets confusing, the hiving off. The historical male and female professions hasn't helped matters.

I was going to ask you about that, your son, and the other man … Ralph, and them both working here. Why?

We're a fifty-fifty employer, as every employer should be, don't you agree?

Morris Law! Of course you're not exempt, I say, remembering how every workplace must now have fifty-fifty representation of the sexes.

My best friend Aprille-Mae has this idea, I say, that with the male suicide rate as it stands, someday we might have to get men from third world countries to impregnate our women. She said we will have to, when the time comes, take Love Holidays.

What an interesting conundrum and a far more interesting resolution, says Pin.

She lifts the page and writes down Love Holiday; the first thing she has written this whole time.

I hope you understand, she says, that I do not hate men. In fact, I rather love men.

Me too, I say, but I can't think of any offhand. On my Love List there is only Aprille-Mae, and at holiday times and birthdays my mother.

So now you'll understand that when I pull up a list of women who are going to get served with Harm Codes that I am not woman-blaming for Jack Henry's behavior.

Who like? I ask.

Well, let me see … there was his first teacher, a woman: Mrs. Ethel Drennan, who awarded him as star pupil, but, in her private notes, stated that she was worried about Jack being on his own with his mother for so long, his father absent.

Oh.

Pin looks at me. Then his second-year teacher, who gave Jack the sports cup. Pin claps her hands.

Timeout: you know, I liked the time when kids weren't all winners and you had to earn your stripes but, to cut a long story short, I can see that young Jack Henry was given an award he did not deserve. The real winner was a girl, they had to give a boy a chance.

Crapola.

Then in high school he really excelled, Jack worked jolly hard but competition was fierce; there were more sad cases; maybe cuter kids who melted the hearts of teachers ... like the young women who left your course.

And Jack?

And Jack – he felt dismayed.

But how do you know?

You remind me of my children when they were younger, says Pin. But *how* are babies made? But *how* does Santa deliver every present to every house all in one night? and I'd tell them, Magic! But this is not magic, Susan, it's just data, and there is a pattern. There are keys for each teacher's agenda, too. Then Jack Henry grows up, and big Jack becomes a brooding, hormonal mess who cannot live with his controlling father. He and his mother have their own secret getaway, but with his father home all the time, Jack cannot prise her away from his side anymore, and Jack is lonely, and seriously starved of affection, now his mother is so devoted and the main carer for his increasingly agitated father, Jack becomes someone else.

This is really helping me understand him, I say.

Don't be one of those people, Susan. He has had tough times and good times, he has a great life over all; I've seen a hell of a lot worse, and so have you. You see, there are women who think they can change men, can help them, heal them. Nurses and teachers, even receptionists, sometimes. The job for the women back then was healing broken men.

He was broken?

He had his mother's secret house and a raging libido and the freedom to bring girls back and he did. Does that sound broken?

You really know all of this?

It's all here. Years of work. Well, says Pin, there were girls who liked him and tried to stick around, like his first wife, Edie; there were women who stuck around and put up with his shit. Like Marlene, his current. Then, there were the others. Pin stops to eat a spoonful of granola.

Girlfriends, I say.

Sometimes not even. Just one-nighters. Pin wipes her mouth. They were girls who couldn't say no, like girls were trained back then. You didn't refuse a man who was smart and strong and handsome-ish, I'd say.

Really?

To avoid the awkwardness. Oh, Susan! They were all called sluts despite being virgins. They really couldn't win.

Sad.

And I can tell you something that will blow you away. Something maybe just as sad.

Go on? I say.

Jack Henry has never brought a woman to orgasm. Not even close.

Are you serious?

Absolutely. It's all there in black and white. Actually a colour pie chart. One colour.

How would you know? I say, dying to know the colour of orgasmless-sex. Too shy to ask.

I told you, he's on the database.

I feel like I didn't need to know that, I say.

Therein lies the problem, Susan. The women he has bedded – and there have been many – thought it an insignificant matter, too.

And, in fact, says Pin, if you were a man drinking in a bar and you got talking to old Jack Henry and you told him that you had made, say, fifty girls come until they cried, old Jack would look you in the eye and hand on his heart tell you that he had doubled your number, and he would not be lying. Not with intention, anyway.

I look at Pin in mortification. I wonder how one hundred women ever fell for his non-existent charm.

It's because, see, if young Jack Henry asked a woman after intercourse if she had a good time, and she said, yes, Jack, because they just said yes back then, then he thought that meant he'd done the business of being a man. To this day he doesn't know his way around a clitoris and Marlene will attest.

You have spoken to his wife?

Not that he asks her these days if she has had a good time, you see, Jack Henry doesn't care. His entitlement is set, his ego is unshakable. But both can be loosened by a day in court, so that's what we're going to do. And right after, all the women who have faked an orgasm with him will have their day. And maybe Marlene will thank us, eventually.

That doesn't seem fair that these women should be charged too, I say.

It will be worth it. We are knocking on the head the very fundamentals that turn men like Jack Henry into selfish, shouty, boring egomaniacs.

But *the women*?

Oh, I see, you think it's all about getting at them, not at all. There are friends of Jack Henry's over the years who have seen the heinous way he speaks to wait staff, and in those cases, it is women. Male wait staff don't make him rage with jealousy quite the same as his students do.

And you will send Harm Codes to his male friends, will you, if they have sat back and not called him out on his horrid behavior?

Jack Henry's friends are all male, of course, and we'll send HCs! says Pin. They might be protected by the Men's Advice Bureau, in which case … we're screwed. But there are some men out there with a conscience and we can try them first.

Great …

So you want to press on?

I don't know, I say, it seems like a lot.

And then I remember how bored and terminally sleepy I have been.

Pin, I do.

Superb, says Pin.

Instructing me in a hopeful outlook she fills a bag with food, hands it to me along with a thick padded envelope entitled *The Grapevine*. Literature, she explains, and don't forget your heart-list.

I hope your daughter enjoys her gift, I say.

I hope she will like them, says Pin, but you just never know. This is the price you pay when you raise girls to speak their mind.

Pin winks then she sees me to the door where her son is waiting to walk me down the corridor, we are halfway down when Pin comes out of her office again and shouts down the hall, I'll email you the name of that cognitive therapist friend, Susan, to help with all your psychological issues.

I try not to die of embarrassment in front of her cute son who is talking to me about the weather and whether I have Christmas plans or not, and who is also telling me to have a great new year, and that he might see me at the party they are throwing in the office, I'd be very welcome, he says as he walks me out to the car park.

I take it *this* is the way younger men know how to talk to women; *this* must be the skill that Jack Henry is so jealous of. And now that I have not been with her for almost a minute I don't know how accurate Pin is anymore, because I am nearly certain that her son is indeed trying – if not in the most polite way ever – to get into my pants. Even a tiny bit.

The woman who accompanied me here nods from her car window and she starts her engine. I feel like I have to follow her and realise when she pulls up outside my apartment that she has been guiding me home. She rolls down her window.

This is for you, she whispers and hands me another envelope which I set on top of the bag of food and the literature from the WAB. Then she takes off and I wait until she is well on her way then I throw everything onto the passenger seat and turn out of the driveway.

I go to my mother's house where I mosey about while she completes chores and I think how much I'll miss and worry about her when I quit my course and leave this place.

Later that night, after I have eaten with her, my father comes in, looks at us with his coked-up eyes, says he's feeling under the weather and goes straight to bed.

Second time this week, my mother says. Fifth time this month. I'll get him a tonic in the chemist and he'll be right as rain for Christmas.

I think she believes in him. I kiss her goodbye and go to my car remembering about the envelope the feathery-voiced woman gave me and I can't believe that for the last few hours I have not thought about it, only about the time I am going to take to work out who I am. What I want.

I open the package and out slides a photocopy of a cherubic baby in a bonnet.

Young Jack Henry is Bonny in his Bonnet, is the headline, and the subhead: *Beautiful baby takes the crown*.

There are his succulent dark cheeks, a grainy, bleached curl peeking out from under a frill of the bonnet. I hold the picture up and try to read what it says beneath, and the words break up and the letters float; I try to stick them back but they have become an equation I can't piece together and the next thing I know I am waking up in my old bed.

When I'm tired and bone-weary, says my mother, I always say *I could sleep for a week*, and you actually did it, Susie. And your father, too. He's been sleeping the clock round.

My mother is telling me that Christmas has been and gone. And she is right. Downstairs the fairy lights are a lacklustre, dead-eyed bracelet. I walk around in a daze, hungrier than I have ever been before. Suddenly, remembering the bag of food on my passenger seat, I tell her I have to get going.

In my car I sit, stuffing stale chocolate cake into my mouth as I leaf through *The Grapevine*. First I look for an index, and the letter I. I for ice rink.

BLACK ICE

AT HOMETIME, THROUGH the crumbling frame of her broken windscreen, Noelle stared back at the Other Mums standing by the school gates. They had to be foundered, standing nude-ankled like that in the snow. All sockless in mock croc skin pumps, their jeggings worming up their legs.

Here even the mums wore uniforms. In springtime it had been Nautical Tops. They'd dismounted their jeeps like a crew of sailors abandoning ship. Had the Other Mums never read magazines? thought Noelle, and therefore missed warnings against horizontal stripes. These warnings were the only thing Noelle remembered about magazines. But maybe the Other Mums were renegades too, in their own obedient ways.

Noelle's Mum Costume was seasonless, old tracksuits she'd kept and renamed Lounge Wear; a 24-hour clothing range with biker boots pulled on over the top. You had to love mornings, when you could drop the kids off at the kerb and stay snug at the wheel in your fleecy dressing gown. In the afternoons Noelle had to get out of the car and join the Other Mums. Thankfully now they knew to keep away and had ceased asking her to join the PTA after what happened last time.

They'd only offered her the position of Treasurer keen to show that even if she judged books by covers, they Did Not. All that money in her care. Didn't Jonny only go and trouser it? After a week of questions, Noelle had to contact that Wee Woman in Donaghadee who arranged loans.

But one Other Mum was undeterred. She invited Noelle and the kids to her home that she'd decorated like a hotel. She'd wanted to show Noelle The Good Life so Noelle would want it herself. Noelle did not.

The Other Mum gave a Ted Talk in the kitchen on The Virtues of Speaking Softly to children:

'They listen better to whispers'

– but when she found her own child pouring beakers of juice without asking for her help, the Other Mum screamed until her face cracked.

Noelle had never seen more sanctimoniousness in her life. Her daughter Smudge took over care of the beakers, unfazed at the screaming, much used to it, unfortunately.

'I swear,' Noelle told Smudge, feeling put on the spot, 'spill that and I'll kill you Stone Dead.'

'Oh, dear, it's just Mi Wadi,' said the Other Mum. 'We don't need actual threats on people's lives.'

'Oh, I'm not really going to kill her,' said Noelle. 'It's called a Figure of Speech.'

This Other Mum worked on obtaining a reciprocal invite which Noelle had no intention of issuing. She was out. What would they say if they saw Noelle's place! The state of her back garden for one, the bottles of drink sitting out, for handiness.

They'd have had her an alcoholic at the school gates. 'It all computes,' they'd be saying, even though their homes had alcohol too and more of it, theirs was hidden away in bespoke bar areas safely away from children, and of course Pretty Storage made all the difference.

After another attempt to sweep away the glass Noelle got out of the car, aware of the stares she joined the Other Mums without exactly joining them. Out flew the kids with Christmas hats on and headbands with pom poms, LED lights flickering and genuflecting, school bags fattened with jumpers, coats tied back-to-front-apron-style around their waists.

'Why is your coat off?' Other Mums said, real annoyed and acting faux-annoyed. 'Oh, I give up.'

Noelle had Given Up. She toyed with the idea of sending her kids in the next day in summer dress and shorts. This would be her Ted Talk: How to Build Your Child's Character.

Kids raised like she raised her kids needed no one's approval. They were Survivors. And she'd send them in in summer uniform too, not least to piss off the teachers.

They'd Given Up too, at last.

Thankfully, the last one had: the Awk-I-Mesh-With-Anyone One who thought she could sweeten Noclle, feeling all Anything is Possible since she'd lost the weight and taken to wearing Lycra – the apparent uniform of Recently Skinnies.

Noelle loathed her most. She was no one's upcycling project.

Handsome came running and hugged her around the hips.

'Alright, Handsome,' said Noelle. She'd always called him that because it wasn't his fault he wasn't.

'Right, Smudge.'

The girl's face was a pleasure but always grubby. She handed Noelle her school bag to carry.

'What happened?' asked Smudge getting near to the car and seeing its every window broken. Soon aware of the slowing queue of rubbernecks, her face pinked.

More glass spilled out when Noelle opened the back door. It was ferocious.

'In youse pop,' she said.

'Is everything alright here?' asked an Other Mum, her eyes dark.

'Everything's the best, and yourself?' Noelle said.

'Do you need me to call the police? What will I say happened?'

The Other Mum's boy ran ahead and tried to open her jeep setting off the alarm.

'Someone's stealing your car! Do you need me to call the police?' Noelle took out her phone.

Did the Other Mum think Noelle had no phone? She had a phone alright. Never credit, but she could take incoming calls. The Other Mum hurried up the lane, bleeping her bleepy thing.

'Wow,' said Handsome peering into the backseats. 'What is This?'

'Are you looking at my crystals?'

'It's broken glass,' said Smudge.

'Nah,' Noelle said, 'crystals. I'm going to sell them like Jack did.'

'Jack?'

'From that panto school took you to see. Remember how he got beans for his cow?'

'They were magic.'

'Well, so are those crystals.' She used the manufacturer's handbook to sweep more curds onto the ground, getting evil eyes left and right.

'What really happened, Mum?' asked Smudge.

'I robbed a jewellery shop for Christmas money, drove into the shop window.'

'No you didn't.'

'Where are our windows gone, Mummy?' asked Handsome.

She thought for a minute. 'Remember your friend's daddy took you for a drive in that car with no roof.'

'Yeah.'

'You liked that, didn't you, wind in your face?'

'Uh-huh.'

'Well, I thought, I want a convertible car, too.'

Smudge shivered. Noelle was freezing now too, she'd felt the cold alright driving out of Belfast towards Newtownards, it was The Shock, then she grew hot with rabid fury, then calmer. You have to be calm for the kids. Don't you?

'Who in the name of God,' her brother said when he saw the car. 'Was it Jonny?'

'Maybe … Indirectly.'

'What does that mean?'

'A friend of his, Not a Friend, someone Jonny obviously pissed off saw my car outside Auntie's.'

'Shit. Where are you going to get the money to fix it?'

'I have a Wee Woman in Donaghadee I can ask.'

He sighed. 'Any sign of Jonny?'

'No, and sure didn't I want him gone?'

'Happy For You and all that, but he still has a duty to the kids.'

Noelle had nothing to say.

'I'll take this to my mate, get his best price for you.'

'Thank you.'

'Does that wee woman in Donaghadee ask for a lot in interest?'

'Less than a payday loan.'

'You'll be paying her off forever.'

'I've no other choice.'

'Bloody Jonny.'

☺

The next day Child Benefit went in. Noelle got credit on her phone and took a bus to the shops. Christmas songs played, all the sad ones, songs Handsome called Lonely. Songs that managed to Resurrect the Dead.

Crossbars of zimmer frames clogged each aisle. Everyone needed and needed now The Thing behind her trolley. Everywhere she stood someone got in her way, in badness, it seemed. It was hard not to Lose One's Shit.

It was true, people went mad at Christmas. When she'd worked here she hated working Christmas. People wanted served quicker than normal, notwithstanding the longer queues, they'd snatched receipts out of her hand and rudely walked away.

'No, thank *you*,' Noelle had shouted after them, only a smidge of aggression in her passive aggressiveness. 'No, *you* have a Happy Christmas.'

That always got a Guilty Glance Back, if you kept your voice upbeat enough.

Aggression had lost all shades of subtlety these days, it was now Postbox Red and spitting feathers. Noelle would never be that rude customer, she'd promised herself, who forgot that cashiers were humans too. She would say Hello and thank them, ask about their day. That was the plan. Noelle forgot it.

In the queue the cashier chatted to the pregnant woman in front as Noelle Tetris-ed the toys and glanced up periodically. The conversation went on after the transaction was done. Noelle sighed loudly, not meaning to. Not able to hold it down.

'I don't know that woman,' said the cashier, feeling she must explain. 'She was telling me she's having baby number six.'

'Mad Bitch,' muttered Noelle.

'Two was enough for me.'

'Too much for me,' Noelle said, complaining But Not Really complaining. Her two were the best mistakes she'd ever made. Where would she be without them?

The cashier scanned the toys and slipped into a trance. Someone behind was right up against Noelle, a hip and upper arm pushing against her. She turned to look, expecting someone who Knew No Better but finding an older woman, designer glasses, fancy clutch bag in her hand, the woman's husband Tetris-ing wine bottles on the belt.

Noelle leaned back, she would not be pushed like this, and she was being pushed. She turned again and came nose to nose with a Real Bad Bitch. Noelle faced away again and stepped backwards, making sure she stood on toes.

'Sorry, I didn't know you were so close – didn't hurt you, did I?'

The woman stared back, recognising a Real Bad Bitch before her, too. Her husband stepped in, incognizant to subtle badness.

'Wild in here today, isn't it?' he said.

'Oh, it is,' said Noelle, 'same every year.'

'Only a week to go,' said the cashier, 'how did that creep up?'

'And yet they have Christmas the same day every year,' the older woman deadpanned.

The cashier half-laughed.

The woman behind pushed against Noelle again.

Harder.

'Sorry,' Noelle said, because people from Ards say sorry but never when something is their fault, only when they are Wholly Not to Fault. 'Do you want past me?'

The older woman glared.

'Or do you want me to bend over and that way you can Crawl Up My Ass?'

The older woman stepped back while her husband stepped forward, opacity clouding his previously see-through face.

'So ... you must have a wee boy and a wee girl,' said the cashier, trying to be friendlier; a Bomb Disposal Technician, like Noelle herself had once been.

'That's not on. I'm going to say something,' the man said.

'Leave it,' said the woman through gritted teeth.

Oh, those teeth, Noelle knew them well. Those teeth had given her pains in the jaw, down the neck, pains that spread upward. They'd evaded Brain Scans, those pains.

'There is no bleeding.'

No bleed, no tumour, no swelling of any sort. The All Clear, they called it. Just a Plain Brain Noelle had. Then she woke one night with a toothache and could not get back over, that was unusual. Even last night, after The Day She Had in Belfast, Noelle slept like a log. After the night of toothache Noelle went to the dentist despite avoiding her for years after cultivating An Irrational Fear, and explained about the pain.

'Your teeth are fine,' said the dentist, 'what you've done is pulled a muscle.'

'Pulled a muscle?'

'In your mouth.'

'Christ,' said Noelle. She wouldn't tell anyone that, it sounded like an occupational hazard for porn stars.

The dentist said, 'Copy me. Do This.' And moved her jaw left. 'Do That.' And moved it right. 'Do This.' Opened her mouth wide. 'And That.' She closed her mouth. 'But Don't Clench Your Teeth.'

Noelle did her workout and the headaches left, along with the toothache.

Now she saw her whole face as a ball of elastic bands.

The cashier was telling her a story about her children, 'Children! They're grown up now ... ' Noelle tried to listen, she moved her jaw from side to side, wide open and closed and looked outside at the snow-swollen sky.

'Think we're due a fresh dose,' said the cashier. 'Nice to see it. Last year was too mild, it Didn't Feel Like Christmas at all.'

The woman behind Noelle was still angering her. Was their showdown over? What was it Jonny learned in that one Anger Management class he bobbed up for, before ducking out, being Not a People Person. Yes, this was it:

'Ask yourself,' he'd scoffed, 'if this will matter in a week's time.'

Would this older woman behind Noelle matter in a week? No. Of course not. By then these toys she was trolleying would be unpackaged parts of the furniture.

The cashier trilled along to Shakin' Stevens. She looked happy, she was Good at Faking It. She had tinsel in her hair, Noelle noticed now, as she took payment, had Noelle swipe her loyalty card and looked right at her, for the first time. There was a flash of distress in the cashier's eyes like a hostage would have; it made Noelle Feel Like Shit. Like a Jonny. Only he never cared enough to Feel Like the Shit he was.

Noelle had a dark compost of thoughts then: starting with Smudge creeping down the stairs and not seeing Mummy Kissing Santa Claus but seeing Daddy Throwing Whatever Came Handy at Mummy's Head or working himself up to. And the rest. Things children shouldn't see.

Handsome always seemed to sleep through, but how could you be sure? And soon he'd be bigger, more easily woken. It would do a boy no good to see his father act in such a way.

Next thought: 'What is that around your eye?' Handsome said, the morning after one such night.

'I'm a panda today,' Noelle told him. She remembered this now, wheeling the trolley out into the snow.

'Then I want to be a panda.'

'No you don't. Pandas eat leaves, they can't have sweets.'

'I want to be a panda.' He'd been about to blub.

'Fine, come here.' Noelle painted around Handsome's eye black and dropped him off at school.

In the afternoon the teacher came out of the gate and said, 'Afraid we have a policy about no make-up.'

'Can I see it?' asked Noelle.

'You may not, because it's not a Written Policy. We simply can't allow make-up for one and Not the Rest.'

This teacher, like Many Teachers, talked to everyone, adults too, like children. Noelle loathed that. She took off her sunglasses, reached into her bag, found Smudge's wet wipes and wiped the correction pen off her left eye. 'Better?' she asked with the shiner exposed.

'Look at Mummy,' said Handsome, 'we are both Pandas today.'

What bloody great kids I have, Noelle thought hauling their toys into the boot of the taxi and onto the back seats. The driver sat watching her from all angles, keeping himself warm. The metre already started. They didn't say a word on the way home.

The Pogues played, then The Waitresses, then Mud. She lugged Every Last Box out onto her empty-bar-snow driveway and posted a tenner through his down-a-crack window.

'No, happy Christmas to *you*,' she shouted as he took off with a skid.

Noelle went round the back to the shed, head down, never looking at that mess of a garden, ignoring it she got the ladder and brought it into the house and up the stairs, then Noelle hauled the toys indoors.

Trembling on the ladder – Jonny's Old Job – she shoved the bags up into the square mouth above her head. Clammily she poured herself a beer after a job well done, then another, since she'd been relieved of driving duties.

She hid the ladder and walked to school, warmer slightly, revived by drink.

As she walked Noelle thought about the Nice Scaredy Cashier. Noelle wondered if she had the patience to work there again. She'd done it before but she'd changed; she had no space for being serviceable anymore. Probably wouldn't last a week in that place.

Crabbit she stood at the school gates.

The Other Mums were in situ, gossiping. They all had their hair up.

That was no good, Noelle theorised. Hair Up meant no sex that night.

And another thing Noelle noticed, if The Husbands ever came to school, say, if it was A Special Day, school play or that kind of thing, the Other Mums' hair would be down, they would be hair-tossing in front of The Husbands. The Husbands didn't seem to notice. They did This School Thing so rarely they blundered about, trying to smile and chat to Other People, even Noelle. Huge mistake.

They didn't know Proper Etiquette about talking only to people who were dressed in the same uniform as their own wives. Avoid Mums in slept-in tracksuits, at all costs.

The Husbands were there to talk to their wife, to Look Lovingly at Her, for the Other Mums to see this walking, talking Instagram. The Husbands would get sex that night for their effort. It was a theory Noelle was proud of.

Only one Husband came to the school gates regularly. Correction: the bench facing it. (Technically an Ex Husband.) He always sat on his bench, looking destructive. The Other Mums pretended he wasn't there. His Ex Wife never did the school runs anymore. But one day, Noelle got there early and nabbed the prime spot so she wouldn't have to leave the car and could stay in her dressing gown, and saw the Ex Wife with a New Fella.

Noelle watched them walk down the lane, then up in front of the school. No one else was about yet. The Other Mums would have loved to see the sunglasses the Ex Wife was wearing: red-framed, heart-shaped.

She was holding this New Fella's hand and with her free hand tried to pull a leaf off a tree and ended up breaking off the whole branch. But She Held On and brought it into the car and waited there for her kids.

Now Noelle stood at the gate and half-listened to the Festive Shit-Chat about Centrepieces for the Table and Garlands for the Fireplace. How the Other Mums' floral-display frivolity bored her!

'They've debt up to their eyeballs, too,' said Jonny once, 'don't be fooled.'

True, they were mums like her, Stay At Homes, but they had what she hadn't now: a man.

If that made much difference!

Jonny's painting-decorating money was always his. And he'd wanted her at home, immured. How would Noelle get a job now anyway with a seven-year hole in her CV?

'Volunteer somewhere, would you not,' Auntie had been saying when Noelle saw that fucker out the front, eyeing the car up.

Noelle was visiting with a tin of petticoat tails and a pretty snow scene Christmas card, quietly cursing the petrol money to Belfast. But she was glad she was free again to see the people Jonny hadn't liked her seeing. Which was everyone, really.

'Volunteer,' said Auntie, 'then someone will give you a reference … '

'A reference,' she tutted, seeing him go, turning back to Auntie. 'I never thought about references.'

'That's why I'm saying, if you volunteer … '

Next he was back, smashing up her wee car.

'What in the name of God in heaven!' Auntie jumped up, Noelle ran to look. He was Going At It with a steering wheel lock, swinging it back, about to do the second window. Noelle bolted outside.

'You Jonny's wife?' he asked. 'Tell him hello.'

She went to run and nearly slipped on black ice. Auntie screamed as the windows exploded inwards. He walked to the other side of the car.

'Stop it!' Noelle screamed. 'Jonny's Gone!'

Next he did the windscreen. 'Call it even,' he said.

She didn't know what this was over but nothing surprised her, Jonny befriended unsavoury types and quickly they unfriended him.

'Car's in getting fixed today,' she said as the kids came out of the school gate. They were not happy to walk. The snow had lost its oddity for the kids.

At least, she thought, they had coats and gloves, and a roof over their heads and toys under that roof. Just as well, because Noelle had nothing left to give away. She'd ebayed old toys, baby stuff, her wedding dress, wedding ring.

It wouldn't matter who came to her door Looking For Jonny, her kids would not go without and that's all there was to it.

She gave Handsome a piggyback ride home, still not used to being in school till 2, his eyes were full of zeds, while Smudge stomped ahead splenetic.

Noelle moved her jaw left and right, opened her mouth wide and closed it.

'Tired, Mummy?' asked Handsome thinking she was yawning.

'Nope,' she said, 'I slept Like A Log last night.'

☺

The next day was a two-hour school day, to watch *Elf* and eat Haribo. Still without wheels she tried to get the time in at the local Garden Centre. To call it a Garden Centre was indeed a cheek, there was a tiny outdoor planty area and indoors, reams of clothes for elderly ladies. Noelle listened to Bing Crosby, Pretenders, East 17, Elton John, and various artists, fondled tree baubles and checked the prices over and over, hoping they'd change. She shunned twelve offers of help by cashiers in the festive spirit, having a Right Old Laugh together. Noelle plucked up the courage to ask if they were looking for anyone.

'You mean staff.'

'Yeah, I mean staff.'

'Not at this time of year, we already have our seasonals, and then it'll go quiet again. If we are, there will be a sign in the window. Keep an eye out.'

She heard the Other Mums coming downstairs, saw those bare ankles, the crocodile stampede. They'd been in the first floor cafe supping cinnamon-spiced skinny lattes, splitting a mince pie seven ways, no doubt.

'I'll keep an eye out,' Noelle said and escaped outside where she stared at the plants.

The automatic doors opened and in came kids with the same uniform as Handsome and Smudge. These kids were older. The school choir, they lined up beside the plants.

The Other Mums followed suit with iPads and a glass of mulled wine that the Garden Centre staff had produced. Noelle sidled over, took a cup and watched the poor half-frozen kids as they sang Silent Night looking ill, infectious and mortified.

Her phone buzzed. Her brother texting that her car was ready.

Whats ur excess?
On my insurance like
Yes, u do have insurance?

It was the first thing to go, first before life insurance, first before home – building and contents. She went outside-outside and phoned him. 'I'll just lift the full whack.'

'Don't tell me you don't have insurance, Noelle.'

'You didn't mention it the other day.'

'Insurance is Not A New Thing. What if you'da had an accident and it was your fault?'

'No more questions at this stage, your honour,' Noelle said and hung up, not in the mood to be lectured, never in the mood For That.

Noelle called the Wee Woman in Donaghadee and told her the sums.

The Wee Woman told her to drive over and collect but Noelle explained she wouldn't have a car until after she had the dough and asked if they could arrange something via Paypal, afraid, because cash Went Like Water through her fingers. But the Wee Woman didn't work like that.

'Can you bring me to Donaghadee first, love?' she asked her brother when he pulled up in his car outside the school.

'You are joking!' he said. He high-fived the kids as they climbed in the back and buckled up.

'Listen,' said Noelle, 'that Wee Woman has mountains of cash in the house. Someone desperate could take advantage.'

'I'm seeing a different side to you lately, lady.'

'How?'

'You sound like *you* want to take advantage of her.'

'Do not!'

'You're getting on like you want to Kill Her and Take Her Money.'

'Mummy doesn't Kill People,' said Smudge, 'it's just a figure of speech.'

He sighed. 'Right, right, I have a bit of wedge on a credit card since I paid my car off.'

'No, no.'

'I insist. Don't even give it back. I've no need for it.'

'Yes you do.'

'Aye, but you're about to do something mad. You have a deranged look in your eye lately, it's since Jonny left.'

'It's just this time of year. Christmas sends people loop-de-loop.'

'It does right enough, but they'll Not Do Without, them two, and that's not what Christmas is about, any road.'

'What is it about?' asked Noelle.

'The baby Jesus!' shouted Handsome.

'And family,' said Smudge, 'and love.'

'Look at her,' said her brother, pulling into the garage, 'wee car's as good as new. Or, good as she was.'

'Can we keep the jewels?' asked Handsome.

'What jewels?'

'Mummy robbed a jewellery shop for gems. That's what was on the floor and the seats.'

'True,' said Noelle. 'Can't lie.'

'You want to watch what you say, he'll go and tell his teacher.'

'He won't.'

'Believe me, Noelle, be careful. The things I've been pulled up on that my kids have made up or I've told them as a joke. Wouldn't take you to be a body with a skeleton.'

At home *Elf* was on the TV. Handsome was happy to watch it again.

In the kitchen Smudge hung about Noelle. 'Mum,' she said, 'after Christmas can I have my room painted pink?'

'You hate pink.'

'No, I hate yellow.'

'You just had it done yellow in November.'

'Can you paint it pink next?'

A bowl of shells still sat by the sink, years on. Smudge had always lifted the spoils of the beach when she was little and said, 'For you, Mummy.' Noelle understood these as priceless gifts. Maybe Smudge would understand.

'Love, Daddy's Away and I have no job, that pays ... I can't do everything. I'd like to but I just can't afford to. I'd get into trouble trying.'

'I won't get you into trouble.'

'I know that. You wouldn't mean to. And Daddy leaving, you know that isn't your fault either.'

'It's yours.'

Noelle felt a jag in the heart. 'No, it's his. Look, we were just fighting a lot.'

'But you ... ' Smudge made a fist and held up her thumb, then ran the thumb along her throat and made a squelch sound. 'You, did That to Dad.'

Noelle felt sick.

'It's okay. I haven't told my bestie,' said Smudge, 'and we tell each other Secrets. But I know this is a Family Secret.'

She gave two thumbs up.

'I don't know what you mean, Smudge. Out of the way, I need to start dinner.' Noelle pulled the chicken nuggets bag from the freezer, her head aching.

'Isn't Daddy dead?'

'Shush! What do you think you heard?' Noelle whispered.

'You saying, "I'll kill you Stone Dead".'

'No, he said that to me. Always saying that to me, so he was.'

'It was you. I thought it was the Christmas tree you were pulling through the garden but I saw the shoes. Behind the shed the next day, I *felt*.'

'What?'

'Laces and ... socks. There was no Christmas tree up yet.'

'Awk, that's been a dream!'

'It wasn't. I touched him with this hand.'

109

She waved a hand in Noelle's face, Noelle caught her wrist then gently released it.

'You know what I love most about you, Smudge, your brilliant imagination.'

'Thank you, Mummy,' Smudge said smiling.

After tea Noelle texted her brother: *One Last Favour?* She told him she had a date.

Where'd u find time 2 meet some1 new?

There were the people who made the mess and the people who always cleaned it up. Right now her brother thought he was the one cleaning up. But really, it had always been Noelle.

'Time you had a bit of fun,' said her sister-in-law at the door as the kids ran off to find their cousins.

'You two go out on Old Year's Night,' said Noelle, 'I'll repay the sleepover.'

She imagined Smudge's pillow-talk with her girl cousins. 'Wanna hear a Family Secret?'

Oh, Christ!

At home Noelle kicked off her high heels, pulled her dress off and Jonny's overalls on. Behind the shed she knelt in the snow and watched for neighbours' lights going on or blinds flickering. No signs of a pulse.

She dug away stones and soil, and quickly found his shoe. Then, down a bit deeper, the other. Unearthed him bit by bit, cocooned in an old duvet cover. She heaved him out, had parked the car as far up the drive as she could get it.

'Just a single mum moving presents around,' she planned to say to neighbours who never showed because no one was home, they were at parties, or out on real dates.

Maybe that would be her in Future Years, came the gust of a thought, while she wheelbarrowed his rigid body to the back of the car where the seats were pushed down flat.

Then Noelle sat in the front, sweating. She wound down the window to let his smell out. The air was static, cold and still. As she drove it began to snow and the town went silent. The tyre tracks were soon covered with snow.

She couldn't deny how pretty everything seemed, looking outward. A Pretty Pollution.

Down by the lough there was snow on the sand. It looked just like a Christmas card.

Holiday Greetings from Newtownards!

FOREVER HOME

AT THE AGE of ninety-eight my great, great uncle Clarence collapsed on his kitchen floor where he putrefied like a banana skin, perishing in the same farmhouse in which he'd been born. An Ards man all his days, he lived near the peninsula, out of town a touch, a wee nudge into the countryside. Not one neighbour within shouting distance.

Not a man I'd ever encountered formally, Clarence was a recluse; a rookish man with fierce nostrils, permanently flared. When I used to see him around the square in my heyday, I'd feel some dark-blooded connection, though I'd not dare tell my friends that Clarence belonged, somewhat, to me. And I dared not believe that I belonged, somewhat, to him.

My mother lived fifteen minutes from Clarence by foot, and had never visited him either. At least not in life. Well-renowned for her skinflintishness, she broke the news of his death to me via WhatsApp.

'You'll need help organising a funeral,' I said, calling her back.

'There'll be no funeral,' she said. The idea bothered me that a life, even one as small, one as unnoticed – as very noticed? – as Clarence's, could slam shut without a bang.

'What is left of our family will get together for a meal,' she compensated.

'Then I'll come home,' I said.

The timing was perfect; I believed I was about to be eradicated by my boss's 'crackers' wife.

Which was how he always referred to her; probably to make me feel better about myself; and to ease my guilt over our involvements.

She had uncovered our hotel receipts, and now, he said, wanted my head on a spike. I can't say I wasn't afraid. I'd seen the 'crackers' wife twice, and remembered most about her that both her earlobes were split.

I often pictured her ripping her earrings out in one of her famous bad-tempered fits.

Now Clarence's demise was my excuse to crawl back to the family and remain there in rent-free safety. My mother was miffed; she saw my life over there as blooming and lush. It really wasn't. Having been sacked, I was sinking in the red.

'It's best you don't work here anymore,' my boss had decided, and since I'd been accountable for half of our predicament, I thought it best not to fight. And anyway, I had never been a fighter.

I booked Cosmo and Misty into a cattery I'd never have to pay for, hoping staff there would take the clue in due course and find the girls a forever home. I hadn't the heart to leave them in a shelter, and maybe it was a bad idea to purchase my flights home with the company card; now the 'crackers' wife might find me. I might wind up facing charges for fraud. But I had little choice, being as broke as I was.

On the flight to London, I tried to settle myself, but when a hand tapped my shoulder, I jumped out of my skin.

'Myself and this young lady,' the male owner of the hand said, 'care to carry on our conversation. Would you mind moving to her seat?'

I had seen them talk in the departure lounge. He had fleshy lips crazed with small cuts. She had frizzy orange hair and oily shins.

Feeling put upon, I moved, and watched the backs of their heads for most of the journey, wondering what two strangers could possibly discuss for all those hours; I never got lost in conversation like that.

My new neighbours were boys, about ten years old apiece. The one nearest to me had a smoker's cough.

'Are you getting sick?' I asked him.

'Him? He always has that cough,' his friend said, leaning in.

Maybe they were brothers; they had the same sharp nose.

I decided there was nothing left to say and covered my face with the complimentary sheet and erratically slept.

When we got to London I was prickly, agitated. Everyone seemed anxious to get up, get out and stretch their legs. We were made to wait before we could alight. I checked my reflection in my phone's selfie feature; there was a hot patch under my chin where I'd held my head up with a fist and sheet scars all over my face.

Flight Information declared the flight to Belfast cancelled.

'We did email you to say,' said the first desk official during our first conversation.

'I was on a flight,' I said, 'I haven't had the chance to check.'

Another official at another desk was adamant the flight would run.

'Go sit by the gate,' he said, annoyed at my disbelieving probings. 'Run! They're about to leave at any second.'

I did run. The flight crew was entering the gate, wheeling their luggage. I told the hostess I was heading for Belfast.

'Ah, that's you,' she said.

They had to go there to come back anyway, and would take me on the flight. She placed me in the middle row to 'balance out the plane'. I sat under polar-cold air conditioning, not a soul beside, behind, or in front of me. A questionable draft puffed in under the door by my legs.

The hostess checked on me.

'This is the first time,' she said, 'in my twenty years working, I've ever had just one passenger. It must be a sign.'

'What of?' I asked.

She didn't say, stacking miniature Coke cans, bags of pretzels, spools of strawberry laces on my tray.

Starving, I ate the lot. My stomach gurgled like a cistern. I felt grateful, but sickly sluggish.

I draped my jacket over my freezing legs. I was too exhausted to sleep.

Then a white line flashed at the corner of my eye and one side of my vision turned violet.

I was up in the air during a thunderstorm I couldn't hear; I only saw lightning as it raced across the sky, turned black to white, white to purple, like a vein pulsing, intestinally alive.

I'm going to die on this flight, I thought then, because I've made some bad life choices, or because I'm running from them, or because my great, great uncle Clarence has died and I have the gall to piggyback on his doom.

Because of the lightning, there was another wait to disembark. My bags never showed at the carousel. Beat, I sat checking my phone for this elusive email from the airline when a WhatsApp message from my mother appeared:

Hurry up!

She refused to pay for car parking.

I didn't report my bags missing or ask for them to be sent to hers. I only wanted my mother; and wanted her to want me, and to see me, her desolate daughter, with nothing bar the smelly clothes on my back.

'You took your time,' she groused.

A wizened old woman was curled in the passenger seat.

'You know your great aunt Edwina.'

I didn't. 'Hello, Edwina,' I said.

Edwina hissed.

At first I tried to be personable, telling them how I'd been the only one on the final flight. They talked among themselves about the wicked weather they'd been hit with, so I let sleep take me until we reached Newtownards, travelling out of the town and up the rise of Movilla, past the hardware shop, past new-build homes that made me feel small because life here had continued without me.

On my right, sat the ruins of the old abbey, the forehead of the cemetery peeking out behind it.

I always pictured the place glossier when I thought of home. It felt like the blood under my flesh. I thought I knew it better than anywhere; than anyone.

Maybe my boss had a point when he'd said, 'I tried to know you, but you don't let people close.'

Well that hurt.

I'd gone over there to find myself but abandoned the mission.

'You can stay tonight, on the air mattress,' my mother said; she lived in the same street and had downsized to an apartment. 'Tomorrow there are people coming to stay after the funeral and I'll have no space.'

'I thought there was no funeral.'

'You know what I mean. Dinner.'

'What about Clarence's house?'

'You wouldn't let a dog stay there,' said Edwina.

'We were there a few days ago,' my mother explained. 'I don't think he'd redecorated since his parents died.'

'I must say,' chimed Edwina, 'all original features. They don't make them like that anymore. You're all of this throwaway generation now.' She glared at me; I thought I saw vicious desires in her.

Edwina took a key from her bag and pressed it onto the table as if it might move.

'The doors are solid wood,' my mother agreed. 'Impenetrable. But you couldn't give them away, so old-fashioned! Not fire regulation either. Told the local charity shop to go in and gut the place out, didn't we, Edwina? They took some things, the rest they said was fit to be burned.'

'Sure, wasn't he dead for months before anyone found him,' Edwina said.

'How *did* they find him?' I asked.

My mother left to locate a pump.

'Did they find him in bed?' I asked Edwina.

It burdened me not knowing whether Clarence died in the sunlight or in the middle of the night.

'Found him sprawled on the kitchen floor, rotted,' she replied. 'You know, you should stay somewhere else. Somewhere nice. What about The Culloden? It's nice.'

She was trying to appraise how wealthy I was; the type of person who believed everyone had secret wealth, somewhere.

'Nice price and all,' my mother called.

She used to distrust banks, preferred to hide rolls of paper money around the old place in little jugs and Chinese takeaway containers.

'I'll find an Airbnb tomorrow,' I said.

'Seems a terrible waste,' said my mother, returning with a foot pump, 'coming all this way for nothing.'

'Not nothing. I get to see you.'

'You'll be heading home straight after the funeral,' said Edwina.

'Will you need a lift to the airport?' my mother asked, hoping not.

'I haven't travelled all this way to go back tomorrow,' I said, affronted. 'I'll probably visit old friends, seeing I'm here now.' I tried to save face.

Edwina quacked with disdain as she slipped away to the spare room, inching towards the mouth-watering bed.

I lifted the long, blackened key and retired to the living room, to stomp my air bed to life. I couldn't stop thinking about Clarence's house; I'd always been drawn to what I ought not to.

Lying on the baggy bed, I added connective tissue to my plan: when the job of doing right by Clarence was done, and everyone had gone, Edwina included, I'd ask my mother if I could move in. What could she say? I was only one person, unimposing, not a stitch to my name.

The next day we three buried Clarence in a family plot.

His mother first, his father second, now in went Clarence with space above him for a fourth.

'Fully paid for.' My mother tittered like a wannabe bride hoping to catch a wedding bouquet.

When we went back to her apartment for dinner and drinks, our company doubled.

All strangers to me, though not to each other. I brought a bottle of wine to the table that would usually last me a week.

A large, older man – an uncle? – reached out and clutched my bottle, lifted it up to the light to read.

When he asked, 'Is this between us?' I came over strange; perhaps I was jetlagged.

'I'd give my last penny to a stranger,' I whispered, 'and would happily share a bottle of wine with a friend, but I draw the line at someone I've known for less than a minute.'

Then I introduced myself and offered my hand. He set the wine bottle down, shook my hand loosely then looked to his plate as my mother spooned out clags of macaroni cheese.

'Don't worry about it,' he said.

I angled myself toward the other stranger on the other side of me, a silent woman with dough-white skin pinched in pie crust rings around her eyes. Five minutes later, a tiny bit guilted, I poured some wine into the man's empty glass.

'Good health,' he said, smacking his lips.

After a dessert of thick-skinned rice pud, a middle-aged man showed up: a distant cousin, I think.

'I didn't see you at the funeral,' I said, following him into the kitchen.

He took a bottle of vodka from his inside pocket and poured himself one straight.

'You might see me later,' he said smiling, showing a forest of teeth. 'I cycle up there.'

'Where?' I asked. 'The cemetery?'

'Once it's closed; it's bloody peaceful.'

'What do you do there?' By then I was not possessive about drink and was working my way down someone else's bottle of Chablis.

'I lie down,' he said, 'and breathe.'

'Well, that's creepy.'

'Sometimes lights float above the graves.'

'Lights? What colour?'

'Sometimes I hear kids laugh.'

'The abbey was a school once,' I said nodding my heavily tipsy head.

'Really?' he asked. 'When was that?'

'The sixth century.'

He laughed.

'You're having me on about the lights,' I said.

'On my life.' He covered his many teeth with his tongue, the vein underneath like a purple rope. 'Have you been?'

'To the cemetery?' I asked. 'Yes, earlier today.'

'No,' he said. 'Before that?'

'We made rubbings of the headstones as kids.'

'Ottilie Patterson's buried over there.'

'Who Patterson?'

'Blues singer. Look her up.'

When he'd cycled off, and every seat in the apartment had an old stranger – or my mother – kipping in it, I walked to the Movilla Road and the cemetery, clambered over the wall. I found a grave for Ottilie by the car park and took a photo of it on my phone.

That phone had survived all sorts: over there it had been lost, found; it had been driven over not once but thrice. But the battery was legendary, it lasted weeks without needing to be charged. At least the last thing I still owned was reliable.

I made my way up the hill, where the open chest of Clarence's grave heaved. I lay down beside it and looked at the stars, waiting for floating lights or the tinkling of ancient children's voices, but instead something dug into my thigh. I put my hand in my pocket and unearthed a key.

It was possible to purchase a croissant and cold latte without being witnessed, I thought as the cashier spilled my change on the counter and turned her back to replenish the tobacco case.

This Spar was Clarence's nearest shop. How many times had he been in here, and had anyone here known him? Would they ever know the erasure of him from their shadow pool of customers? I couldn't get the man off my mind.

Bypassing turtle-shaped droppings in the dark, I made my way up the lane to his farmhome. The face of it looked slack and appalled; the windows were undersized eyes. First I struggled with the lock, then shouldered my way in through a rocket-heavy door. The living room teemed with knick-knacks that teemed with dust; and already my throat itched.

There were cracked leather seats that had buckled and the floor had become its own animal, dense with the pelts of pets Clarence had once owned, or imprisoned.

In the kitchen, I left the cold latte and the croissant on the counter for breakfast, then searched by my feet for the stain of his death and found it. Gross, yes, but maybe it wasn't so bad. A place for the night, or maybe I could clean it up in the morning, give it a go. Who would think to look for me here?

I thought of Clarence spending his first night in his new home in the earth, and the company he had now that he never had before. I wondered if he'd like that. But as a recluse I knew he wouldn't. At least it was good company. I thought of Ottilie Patterson. Then I remembered my boss's password for a music streaming service, and on my faithful, old phone Ottilie Patterson lived on. So I played *Make me a Pallet on the Floor*: which was an old bluesy number, soulful, upbeat with a little menace, and I found I was partial to it, blasted it hard and began to sway about.

When it ended, I put the song on repeat while I checked jugs and containers for more than buttons, snapped curtain hooks and open-pronged safety pins, on which I must have pricked my finger because it dripped with blood, but I, still drunkish, felt nothing.

Sucking my finger, I went in search of a bed and a bed I found. But the bedding was like card and the base had cowped. And upstairs, the whole place was shadows and whispers, and gave me the heebie jeebies, big time.

I pictured Clarence skulking around, grumbling, nasally breathing, nostrils flared. The floorboards creaked at the end of the landing. I swore a darkening in the hall was him. Enough madness! I had seen him lowered into the ground.

I decided I'd go back to my mother's and explain that I needed a bed, say I'd kip anywhere, in her car, in the bath, until her visitors were gone. I'd beg.

But first, my bladder was a swelling balloon I considered holding on to until I got to my mother's, but I had to let go, making a dash for the bathroom, slamming the door, and, out of habit, locking it.

Not letting the cold, sticky, furry, porcelain bowl touch against my skin, bow-legged I squatted. Then I could find no loo paper, just a puff pastry of paper squares like the ones you find in fruit crates. Then I shivered and wiped. Hummed to myself as Ottilie warbled on.

I went to wash my hands but the sink faucet was stuck, the bath faucet too. Even the flush didn't work.

I was alone in a desert; a thick, furry, dusty, deserted desert.

I caught a cough at the back of my throat and grew hot in the head.

Make me a Pallet on the Floor was starting over, the clear notes were bent by the solid door. I hummed along, wiped my hands, that bloody finger, on my trousers, then made to leave but no amount of shoulder charging the door would let me out. No amount of fiddling with the handle would offer release. There wasn't a coat hanger to jigger about the lock. No phone in my pocket, where it usually lived.

Five crispy flies lay on the window ledge. One brute-strong window above them. I could just about open it an inch. I could stand on the cracked toilet lid and bootlessly scream. Not one soul would hear.

Provision was first published in the Honest Ulsterman.

Black Ice was first published in *Underneath the Tree*.

Thank you to my family, friends and writing community for all their support.

This collection was published with the support of the Arts Council of Northern Ireland's Support the Individual Artist grant.

'I hate flowers – I paint them because they're cheaper than models and they don't move.'

– Georgia O'Keeffe

Printed in Great Britain
by Amazon